D1824894

The Bridge of Shadow

The Bridge of Shadow

Creativia Anthology II

Edited by Natalie J Case

Acknowledgements

As always, a book doesn't appear in a vacuum. I'd like to acknowledge the cheerleaders who keep me going, even when I feel like I've bitten off way more than I will ever be able to chew. You all know who you are, and I love you more than you will ever know.

Forward

This is our second anthology for Creativia Publishing working off the same premise: give the 100+ authors who write for Creativia the same prompt, and no other rules but for minimum and maximum word counts and give them a couple of months to noodle over it to come up with their own interpretation of that prompt.

This time around, our prompt was: The letter/email/missive/-message was ominous, if a little vague in the details. "Midnight, on the bridge. Come alone."

The important thing in a challenge like this is to honor the essence of the prompt, and mold it to fit into the story you are set to tell.

Once again, my fellow authors did me the honor of submitting stories that cover a broad swath of genres and themes: love stories, mysteries with a taste of history, cautionary tales of late night meetings with attractive men, sentience in unusual places, magic animals and a taste of the paranormal.

Thank you, Creativia for affording me the opportunity to pursue this wacky idea, and thank you authors for trusting me with your words!

Natalie J Case
Editor

Contents

Croatoan

Craig Gaydas

Roanoke Island, North Carolina, August 1590

"The evening creeps closer as we come to anchor near the Hatteras Islands. Off in the distance we can see smoke rising on the isle of Roanoke near the place where I left our colony in the year 1587. The smoke gives me hope that the colony is still present, expecting my return out of England."
– *Journal entry, fifteenth of August, 1590, John White*

He closed the journal and cupped his head in his hands. Sitting behind his desk aboard the British privateer ship, *Moonlight,* he concentrated on the sounds of waves crashing against the hull, a sound which always put his mind at ease. He longed to reunite with the colonists on Roanoke Island but was even more eager to be with his family again. His granddaughter had been only nine days old when he departed the settlement and sailed back to England and his heart yearned to hold her once again.

"This cursed war with the Spanish set me back years," he grumbled.

Through the door, White watched Captain Lane descend the stairs leading to his quarters with his gaze fixed upon John. The look was filled with frustration mixed with relief, a look only the captain could mix into a single facial expression. The return voyage to Roanoke had been long and difficult, rife with frequent storms and rough seas which battered the ship into near obliteration. Coupled with occasional pirate skirmishes along with navigating away from their normal course in efforts to avoid the Spanish Armada had taxed their supplies, along with their patience. They had run dangerously low on fresh water, rations and time.

"Sorry to disturb you but I wanted to report we have spotted smoke rising from island in the area near the settlement. Unfortunately, this darkness is so thick I could cut it with a dagger which makes navigating this damn ship about as easy as gathering a flock of headless chickens. I'm sorry to report the weather conditions will delay us setting ashore this evening," Lane stated flatly. Lane did not share John White's desire of reuniting with the colonists of Roanoke Island. He was a great navigator, but his only incentive during this expedition was the gold the crown fed into his purse.

"I agree," John replied with a hint of resignation in his voice. "What's one more day? For safety's sake let us disembark first thing in the morning."

Lane turned and lumbered up the stairs. Faintly, he could be heard barking orders to the deckhands before the rattling of the lowering anchor drowned out the voices. Once the anchor stopped the captain's heavy footsteps could be heard as he trailed off toward his quarters.

John laid upon the bed and rested his head on the feathered pillow. Despite their differences in opinion he had a lot of faith in the captain's abilities. Captain William Lane was one of the best ocean navigators the Crown could buy. His battles with the Spanish Armada were stories of legend and his ability to fend off pirates had been an extremely valuable commodity. His familiarity with voyaging across the Atlantic had been an added bonus, but it took a lot of persuasion, and coin, to persuade him to agree to lead this dangerous expedition. Even if one were so inclined to remove the Spanish Armada and piracy from the equation, Roanoke Island was currently in the midst of peak hurricane season, making navigation difficult. White had been contemplating how much gold this latest delay would cost before sleep finally took hold.

The shuffling of feet from above his cabin woke John from his slumber. The splash of an anchor could be heard as it was raised from the sea. The ship started to drift closer to the island which elicited a small grin from John. The strong smell of the Atlantic air drifted into his cabin and filled the cramped quarters. John grabbed his journal and sprinted up the stairs, nearly bowling over Captain Lane in the process.

"Good morning Captain," John beamed. "I assume we will be disembarking this morning?"

"Aye. I have commanded our master gunner to prepare our two minions and our falcon and make sure they are well loaded. They have orders to fire signal shots with reasonable space between each shot, so the colonists are prepared for our arrival. We should be ready to drop anchor soon."

"Great idea, Captain! I assume you will be accompanying us to the colony?"

The captain's reply was as flat as his demeanor, "Aye." He glanced toward the deckhands preparing supplies and loading them into the sloops which would carry them to shore. "I assume we won't need many provisions as the settlement has ample supply?"

"Yes Captain," replied White. "There is no need for you to stay longer than necessary. Once we verify the colonists are in good health and the supplies are sufficient to last through the winter, you are free to return to England."

It took roughly three hours to load all of the supplies. John glanced upward and noticed the clouds darkening with a slight increase in wind from the northeast—a sign of an impending storm. He looked at Lane who squinted against the fading sun

"We better head out," muttered a wearied Lane. "It seems we might be in for a bit of a storm."

Lane and White set sail from the *Moonlight* with a crew of eleven. As they approached the island Lane pointed toward the area where smoke had been visible earlier. "We will land there," he explained. "That's the most likely position of your colonists."

"I agree, Captain. As we get closer I will sound the trumpet for the savages."

Savage had been a term used by the colonists to refer to surrounding indigenous tribes located on Roanoke Island as well as the neighboring barrier islands. It had been customary for the English to sound a trumpet to announce their arrival to the inhabitants. Between the trumpet and cannon fire, White knew the colonists would not mistake him and the crew to be savages, pirates or hostile Spaniards.

The boat landed about a half mile from where the smoke had been spotted. As soon as the boat touched the sand, White blew the trumpet. Lane and crew exited the boat and gathered the supplies. As two of the sailors struggled unloading a cask of fresh water, Lane touched White on the shoulder.

"I don't see any sign of your colonists, John. Why do they not set out and meet us, or at least acknowledge the call?"

White shrugged, wondering the same. The only signs of activity along the shore were a few footprints in the sand. White leaned over and grimaced as he examined them.

"Savages," Lane confirmed over John's shoulder. "Not uncommon for this part of the island."

"No, this was not an uncommon thing." White replied. As a matter of fact, before John left, the colonists had made peace with the locals and had begun trading with them. Right before White left for England, there had actually been discussions about relocating the settlement to nearby Croatoan Island.

As the group moved further inland, they stumbled across the source of the smoke. A fire had been abandoned, nothing more than smoldering ashes. Lane kicked at a pile of rotten tree limbs piled alongside the fire and frowned. "What do you make of this? It's strange to have an unattended fire located so far from the settlement, is it not?"

"It's uncommon, yes," White replied. "However, look at these tracks running alongside the shore line. These are native tracks." The Croatoan tribe were the only tribe who inhabited the barrier islands. The fruits of the sea attracted them, and they had been drawn toward the beaches, while other tribes chose to maintain their settlements and villages further inland. It was not rare to see their tracks so close to the settlement, however, some mainland tribes were at odds with the Croatoan tribe and did not look upon them favorably.

"Let's move further inland, Captain," White said as he turned to Lane. "We should take some provisions with us, just as a precaution." Lane nodded his head in agreement. He turned and motioned to the sailors remaining in the boat.

The group ventured about a mile and a half inland where they came upon a large wooden fence constructed from logs surrounding the entire settlement. The fence was sturdy, and had been erected as a defensive structure rather than a cosmetic one. Beyond the fence, the settlement appeared to be undisturbed with the exception of the houses. Most of the houses sheltering the colonists had been taken down. There appeared to be no signs of a battle or any sort of struggle. As the group moved into the settlement they stumbled across cannonballs, iron bars and other such heavy metal objects scattered around the area covered with so many weeds that the foliage nearly hid them from detection.

"What in the bloody hell?" Lane exclaimed, surveying the settlement. "Where are your colonists, John?"

John was dumbfounded. In a panic he hurried to where his daughter' house had been established. When he arrived his shoulder slumped in dismay when he saw that it had been taken down just the rest of the colony. Where the house once stood was nothing but the scattered remains of his personal belongings. On the ground nearby lay a suit of armor that was nearly devoured by rust lying beside various pictures and frames that had been scattered and broken. Maps and charts of the surrounding islands sat rotted and destroyed by the weather. Various chests that had been buried for security reasons had been dug up and ransacked. When John turned to Captain Lane, his face paled considerably.

"It seems the savages have ransacked what was left of the colony," White acknowledged. "But I don't understand why there are no signs of a skirmish. There are no signs that the colonists had defended themselves or put up a fight in any way with the exception of the bloody wall. It makes no sense!"

Lane's mouth formed a thin line of dismay as he examined the area. "I agree with your assessment. All of the footprints appear to be recent and are definitely made by locals. If there were any colonist tracks in the sand, they must have been washed away by the rains." Lane turned to White. "The evidence points to the savages entering the colony *after* the colonists had departed the area. There are no bodies, blood nor scorch marks from fire. I do not see any arrows, spearheads or discarded weapons anywhere. It also appears the houses had been taken down with precision which leads me to believe the colony was not removed by force."

White nodded in agreement. "It is entirely possible they moved to another location. I instructed them if they decided to relocate that they would carve into a nearby tree clues to their new destination." White looked at the tree line bordering the settlement. "Come, let's check those trees over there. If the colonists moved then those trees may provide the answers we need."

White and company gathered near the trees bordering the forest. After inspecting several trees, one of the sailors shouted. "Over here, Captain!" White and Lane hurried toward the frenzied man.

Located about half way up an old cedar tree a large portion of bark had been removed. Upon the tree carved in large capital letters stood the word: **"CROATOAN"**. Lane looked toward White with a quizzical expression on his face. "John, do you think this means your colonists have moved?" He motioned toward the direction of the neighboring Hatteras Island, also known as Croatoan Island. "Perhaps we should head to the inlet to see if their boats are gone?"

White nodded in agreement although he did not move. He continued to study the word carved into the tree. The carving did not seem forced or in distress, and the letters were as clean and legible as could be, as if someone casually carved while they leaned against the tree. The colonists had been instructed if they were ever attacked or forced to relocate they would attempt to carve clues into trees with the symbol of a Maltese cross. Upon further searches of the area, no one could find any further clues or carvings. Eventually White abandoned his search and turned to the group.

"Yes, let's check to see if the boats are still anchored nearby," he agreed.

The group made the short hike to the inlet in silence. John's thoughts were focused solely on the fate of his family while Lane continued to check his portable sundial. He realized he would need to depart soon if he were to stay ahead of the approaching storms, but he also knew the importance of locating the missing colonists. When they finally reached the inlet, John's expression turned grim. Anchored nearby were the two small boats left behind by the colonists. Lane approached the nearest skiff and peered inside. Everything seemed to be normal. There had been weather damage to the boats, one had even been beached, but there were no signs of aggression or vandalism to either boat. Lane realized this past year has been dreadful in regard to hurricane season so he could only imagine how three years of weather damage would have taken a toll on the vessels, but they still remained seaworthy. Lane motioned toward the boats. "It appears the colonists have not left the island in some time, at least not in these." He kicked at a single plank that had broken off the beached boat and looked up. The sky grew an ominous gray-purple color and began swallowing the setting sun, the sign of an approaching storm. "Listen, John. It appears your colonists have moved on to one of the barrier islands. I hate to cut this adventure short but if we do not set sail soon we could be stranded for days."

White's frustration was palatable. "Aye, Captain. Let us collect what we can salvage and head back to the ship." He turned and walked away.

As they returned to the settlement, Lane barked orders at the sailors to collect any useful salvage and load it onto the boats. They made their way through the camp and it wasn't long before Lane realized the savages took anything of use. The only thing his crew could salvage were some iron bars and a handful of cannonballs.

"Damn savages," he muttered. He boarded the boat and looked back to see John peering into the forest with a queer look on his face, as if he were in some sort of trance.

"John, are you alright?" Lane asked while approaching him cautiously.

"Huh?" he responded sleepily. "Oh yeah, I'm ok. I just get this uneasy feeling when I look at the forest." He continued staring into the thick tree line calmly and Lane's eyes drifted toward the spot of John's interest.

"Savages?" Lane asked.

John shook his head. "I don't believe so. We are a small group, if savages were watching us they would have either attacked or approached us with curiosity, depending on the tribe." He turned and boarded the boat but couldn't shake the feeling he saw something in the woods. The hair on the back of his neck stood firm.

"Take us back to the ship!" Lane barked to the sailors. The ship drifted away from the island and he noticed White's gaze still fixed upon the forest. Lane wasn't sure whether the man was upset at the fact the colonists were gone or the strange feeling that came over them at the edge of the forest. He decided to let it go.

They boarded the *Moonlight* and Lane commanded a nearby sailor to raise the anchor. While glancing at the darkening sky with dismay the wind picked up which filled him with concern. "John, we won't be able to search Croatoan Island. It seems a squall is blowing in from the northeast. We need to return to England now or we are in danger of spending days on these islands. Normally a few extra days on the island wouldn't be anything more than an inconvenience, but with the colonists deconstructing the colony, they left us with little shelter. I know that's not what you want to hear but it's either we leave or risk being dashed upon the rocks."

"Aye, Captain. I will be in my quarters if you need me," White grumbled.

Lane watched as the man descended the stairs to his quarters and couldn't help but think about the look that had been pasted on White's face when he stared into the forest. Lane returned to his quarters and sat upon the bed, replaying the look in his head. He leaned back and stared at the ceiling. It was only after his eyes closed that he recognized the emotion on White's face. It wasn't despair or concern for the lost colonists. It had been fear. But fear of what? Certainly not of savages since White had spent years on the island with them and had been used to their behaviors. Something spooked White, something having to do with the colony's disappearance. "What do you think happened to them, John?" he whispered to the darkness before drifting into sleep.

"The eighteenth of August. Captain Lane and I have agreed that due to extreme weather conditions we will set sail for the island of St. John's. We are running low on fresh water and the storm damaged two of our anchors. We came perilously close to being run aground near Hatteras Island. The storm battered the ship like a ram against a gate. I mourn the fact I was unable to reunite with my family or my brethren on Roanoke Island and I can only hope and pray they are safe."
  -John White

He closed his journal and put his head down. The queer feeling of being watched on the island still haunted him. The word "**CROATOAN**" haunted him. When he first spotted the word he thought their disappearance could easily be explained; the colonists simply left the island for Croatoan Island. The boats still present, however, removed the simplicity of the situation. His brow furrowed as he struggled to remember something learned while living among the natives. It had something to do with a legend passed down by their Algonquin ancestors. He recalled rumors spreading amongst the settlers regarding the other tribes resorting to cannibalism. Food supplies had been running low among them and they became desperate. There had also been an old Algonquin tribal legend which spoke of demons possessing people causing them to feed on human flesh. These poor souls would forever roam, eternally seeking new victims to feed upon since their hunger would never be sated.

"No that can't be!" White muttered to himself. "There were no signs of that sort of thing happening to the Roanoke settlers!" *Cannibalism*? He had never witnessed such a thing in all his years spent among the tribes or the settlers. Doubt began to creep into his thoughts as he remembered a discussion he had with one of the tribal elders. The elder stated that some of the hostile tribes along the barrier islands began eating each other because their food sources had all but vanished due to an unusual drought that ravaged the area. He mentioned the demon legend and believed these foul creatures were somehow conjured by the island tribes to seek out food sources. Other tribesmen claimed they had witnessed these beasts before, describing them as having hearts of ice with claws as long and as sharp as spears. Their teeth, pointed and equally as sharp, burned like hot irons when biting into one's flesh. The Algonquin had a name for this monstrous spirit of darkness. They referred to it as a Wendigo.

"Wendigo." The word slipped from his lips like a fine mist. Surely the tales had been meant to scare the children and curious settlers, but he could not shake what he saw within the depths of the forest, peering from the trees. His thoughts drifted to the pair of scarlet eyes fixed on their group as they left the colony. Surely, he did not imagine the tall gaunt figure moving from one tree to another, eyeing them hungrily. John refused to tell the captain about what he saw for fear the privateer would think he had gone mad. The tribal word continued to float through his mind like a piece of driftwood.

Wendigo.

* * *

Bodie Island, North Carolina, August 1993
August 30th, 2:00 pm

"*The National Weather Service has issued a hurricane warning for Eastern North Carolina, The Outer Banks, Virginia Beach as well as Delaware and Maryland coastal areas. Damaging winds, severe flooding, and loss of power are expected within these areas. The Governor of North Carolina has issued a mandatory evacuation for low lying coastal areas. Stay tuned to this channel for further updates and instructions.*" -WTVR News, North Carolina.

August 31st, 5:00 pm

"*Hurricane Emily has made landfall off of the coast of North Carolina. According to the National Weather Service, The hurricane is currently a Category Two storm and as such, residents are to remain indoors or at their current evacuation points until the storm passes over. There are reports of three to five foot storm surges off of the coast near the town of Buxton as well as over seven inches of rain. News reports have reported sinkholes in the area south of Buxton along Highway 12. Residents who have not evacuated are urged to remain indoors as there are also reports of downed power lines. The storm is expected to make landfall as a Category Three. Stay tuned to this news station for further updates and instructions.*" -WTVR News, North Carolina.

September 1st, 11:35 pm

"Hurricane Emily has moved out of the Outer Banks and appears to be heading north towards Virginia. Early reports state that the damage along the Outer Banks is catastrophic." Ted Koppel announced to the television audience. *"As of right now we have lost contact with several correspondents due to the power outages. Early reports are estimating preliminary damage around thirty-five million dollars. Local news agencies report two deaths along the Nags Head coastline. Over 160,000 people have been evacuated along the North Carolina barrier islands. I urge residents to remain at home and off the roads to allow emergency crews to do their jobs."* -James Hunt, Governor of North Carolina

What the Governor did not realize was something else happened during the storm. With all things considered it was relatively unimportant in regard to the storm itself, but the impact of events could not be denied. Along the coast of Bodie Island, near the keeper's quarters of the lighthouse serving as a beacon for ships passing thru the inlets of the barrier islands, something long forgotten had been unearthed. On the coast of Lighthouse Bay washed ashore a small wooden chest not much bigger than a toaster, battered by hundreds of years of weather and time. The chest landed on shore and came to rest along a stony embankment, but the storm was not done with its plan for this particular piece of ancient debris. The gusts of wind accompanying the storm actually launched the chest into a sinkhole where it came to rest within the center like a perfect hole-in-one. It was either by natural or supernatural forces (which are still debated to this day), huge chunks of wood and concrete debris that had been tossed around by the storm filled the hole and covered the chest where it would remain. It was not meant to be discovered.

Yet.

* * *

Bodie Island Lighthouse, May 2011

Vinnie was suffering a tropical storm-sized headache that was slowly morphing into Hurricane Migraine. The restoration of the Bodie Island Lighthouse was taxing his patience as well as his budget. Two years ago the National Park Service approved the work of restoring the cast iron and masonry of the lighthouse including the structural work of the keeper's quarters, however Vinnie and his crew continued suffering challenges on a daily basis. Work had to be stopped last year due to structural deficiencies associated with corrosion of the metal on the lighthouse gallery and lantern levels. Vinnie strolled along the bypass road near the keeper's quarters, pondering how he could weasel out of this job and into early retirement when all of a sudden he heard a thud and a shout.

"GODDAMIT!"

Vinnie hurried to the southeast side of the building where one of his crewmen, Steven Grayson, was stuck halfway into the ground roughly twenty five feet from the entrance to the lighthouse parking area.

"Jesus Christ, Steve hold on I'm coming." Vinnie grabbed him by the wrists and pulled. The man popped from the hole like a cork from a bottle.

Both men fell backwards from the momentum. With the exception of a few cuts and bruises Steve appeared unhurt.

"My ribs hurt like a son of a bitch," Steve grunted.

"What the hell happened?" Vinnie asked.

Steven stood up with a grumble and brushed himself off. "I was heading to the truck to get another trowel because either the crew keeps stealing the damn things or this lighthouse is eating them. I was walking across what I thought was just a pile of debris when I fell straight into this hole!"

"Well are you ok?" Vinnie asked. "You know this project has been a nightmare and I can't afford you taking time off and sucking the teat of the worker's compensation program."

Steven saluted with his middle finger. "You know I'm the only stonemason worth a damn in this state. If I was out, you would be trying to put this place together like Lego with your thumb up your ass."

Vinnie grunted. Steven was examined the hole and turned to Vinnie. "Hey you got a flashlight?"

Vinnie fumbled around in his back pocket, brought out a mini Maglite and handed it to him. "What do you see? Please tell me it's buried treasure and maybe I'll cut you in some."

Steven grabbed the flashlight and struggled to see down the hole, ignoring the quip. He pointed the beam of light towards the center of the hole. "Hey, Vin, check that out. You see that?"

Vinnie peered into the hole. At first he could see nothing but gloom, but as his eyes adjusted he noticed the flashlight beam reflecting off of an object. It seemed to be a wood container about the size of a small microwave located at the bottom. "Help me move some of this debris out of the way so I can reach it."

They cleared some of the larger tree branches and a large portion of the chunks of stone that blocked access to the object. Despite his best efforts Vinnie couldn't quite reach it. It appeared his love of New York style pizza prevented him from reaching the object without some sort of excavation equipment. He looked over to Steven who was slim enough to reach it. "Hey Steve, apparently I need a diet. Do you think you can reach it?"

Steven grunted and rolled his eyes. "Time for a diet, fatty."

Vinnie had to resist the urge to shove Steven into the hole. Steven squatted and entered the hole while Vinnie grabbed his ankles and helped lower him into the hole. Even with Steven's slim physique it was still a struggle to get him into the hole.

Steve gripped the object and made sure it was secure before calling out. "Ok Vin, go ahead and pull. I got it."

Vinnie pulled and with some effort dragged him out. When the man popped from the hole he lost his grip on the object and it landed nearby in the grass. As soon as Vinnie saw it he immediately remembered a scene from *Raiders of the Lost Ark* where Indy and his lady friend were tied up and the bad guys were about to open the Ark. The chest resembled a wooden miniature replica of that box. They both approached the object cautiously.

Steven gawked at the object. "Hey that thing looks old, do you think it might be worth something?"

Vinnie studied it. He knew nothing about old stuff like this. He was a construction worker not an archaeologist. He ran his hand across its surface. "Well let's see what is inside." He gripped the lid from a corner and tugged but the lid didn't budge. "Hey Steve, can you run to my truck and grab a flat head? This lid is stuck."

Steven returned with a flat head screwdriver. He handed it to Vinnie and started drooling at the thought of some sort of ancient treasure pouring out of it as soon as the lid was opened as if it were some sort of ancient piñata.

Vinnie stabbed the top of the box with the screwdriver. At first the lid refused the screwdriver's advances, but he added some extra elbow grease and eventually the lid popped off. The men shoved at each other to get the first glimpse of the contents.

Inside the box was a leather-bound book. Vinnie grabbed it and turned it over in his hands. Upon closer inspection it seemed to be a journal of some kind. He glanced at Steven who looked as if someone punched him in the gut. "Not much in the way of gold and jewels, huh?"

"Nope, not really," acknowledged Steven. "Might as well open it and see what's inside."

Vinnie opened the journal. The words appeared to be an older version of English. There were several words spelled incorrectly with either an extra *e* or a random *y*. "Well the book seems to be old," he admitted. "A lot of these pages are worn and strange looking. Not like paper you see nowadays." He turned to Steven. "I guess we should call someone and let them know what we found."

"Maybe we should call the police, in case this belongs to someone. I don't want to get pinched for stealing," Steven replied.

When Vinnie nodded in agreement, Steven grabbed his cell phone and dialed the Dare County Sheriff's Department. The dispatcher advised that an officer would be along within the hour. Vinnie supposed a box found in a hole didn't signify much of a priority for the Sheriff's Department.

They were in the middle of a debate on how they would tackle the problem with the masonry work at the base of the lighthouse when a dark colored Ford Crown Victoria pulled up. The driver door opened and out stepped a thin, blond haired man with glasses who looked more suited for the engineering department at Wake Forest than the Dare County Sheriff Department. The deputy approached the men and introduced himself.

"Hi, I am Deputy Michael Schraeder from the Dare County Sheriff Department. I hear you guys found something strange?" he asked in a deep voice that belied his physique.

"Yes sir. My name is Vinnie Rouse and this is Steven Grayson. Steve here managed to get stuck in a sinkhole and after pulling his dumb ass out, we found this." Vinnie handed the book over to the cop, but didn't miss the irritated look Steven tossed him.

The investigator took the book and flipped through the pages. "Hmm, a lot of these words are strange, sort of like reading Shakespeare." His glance drifted away from the pages and towards the men. "Dispatcher said you found a box?"

Steven handed the box over to the cop. "Here is the box, and it looks old. But it seems to have held up over the years pretty good."

The deputy placed the book inside the box. "Well here's the deal. There isn't much we can do since nothing like this has been reported stolen. Stuff like this just ends up in the property room collecting dust but since this appears pretty old, I have a cousin at Brenau University who is a professor of anthropology. If anyone is able to identify this and figure out where it came from, it would be her. Let me take down your contact information so if she has any questions she can contact you directly."

After jotting their information into his notepad, Michael placed the box in the back of his vehicle, got inside and took off. During the return trip to headquarters, he flipped open his cell phone and dialed his cousin. After three rings a pleasant voice on the other end answered. "Brenau University Anthropology Department, this is Professor Barbara Perkins, how may I help you?"

"Hey Barbara this is Mike," he responded. "Sorry I have to make this brief because I have some reports that need to be completed before the end of my shift. Earlier today, two guys working construction at the Bodie Lighthouse found something you might be interested in. It looks like an old chest with a book inside. The words on the pages appear to be something straight out of a Shakespeare novel. Do you mind if I ship this down to you and see what you can make out of it?"

"Well hello to you too, Mike!" she replied. "Go ahead and ship it over here and mark it to my attention so it makes its way to me. Make sure my name is on the package or the morons at the front desk will never get it to me."

"Thanks, cuz." Mike said. "I will ship it out today and you should have it in a day or so. Say hello to Brian and the kids. Sorry to be so brief, but I promise to schedule a get together soon."

"I look forward to it," she replied.

* * *

Two days later she was still thinking about what Mike had said. *The words that are written in it appear to be something straight out of a Shakespeare novel.* A book found off the coast of North Carolina with this style of language can only be from the Renaissance era. She originally thought of a Civil War journal but the fact it was inside a chest made her think otherwise. She could hardly contain her excitement and anticipated the arrival of this new find. She was sitting behind her desk working on the final parts of the exam she would unleash upon her students when her phone rang. She answered on the second ring and a voice on the other end said, "There is a package for you at the front desk, Professor."

Barbara practically tripped over herself getting to the front desk. Sitting beside the desk was a package roughly the size of a microwave. "Can I borrow your cart, Bill?" she asked the front desk guard. He rolled over a steel frame cart used for hauling school supplies back and forth. She loaded the package onto the cart and returned to her office. She gently picked up the package and placed it on her desk and with careful precision sliced the top of the box open with a box cutter. She removed the book and set it carefully beside the box.

"Well look what we have here." She admired the chest which had been battered by time and weather but sturdy and still relatively intact. The ancient craftsmanship of the chest was marvelous she acknowledged as she slowly walked around it. She ran her hand over the recessed flat tops and curving acanthus leaves adorning it. Her eyes widened when she noticed the sides revealed the influence of classical Roman sarcophagi. The chest had also been decorated with bizarre masks and strange figures with elegantly contorted forms typical of chests from the Renaissance Era. This chest seemed to be Italian made and carved from a single tree trunk. Her curiosity switched to the book lying beside the box.

As soon as she flipped through the pages she realized it was a journal or codex of some kind. The book, bound in vellum with pages made from an ancient parchment material, confirmed the authenticity of the find. As she browsed the pages of the book she was ecstatic when she noted a date written on the first page; *1589*. A journal from the New World! She could hardly contain her excitement. As she read through the pages she realized that translation from the old English would take some time.

It took Barbara about four hours to finish the translation. When finished, she laid down the pencil and stared at the words she had wrote. She would have probably been done in under two hours, but she couldn't believe some of what had been written. She needed to double and triple check her work to make sure what she was writing was accurate. "This is big," she muttered to herself. What she had just translated had great historical implications. If the journal was to be believed than a consultation with a historical expert would need to be done in order to verify their authenticity. She scooped up the journal as well as her translations and ran down to the office of Professor Stan Michalek, the resident history scholar at Brenau. She burst through Professor Michalek's door and took a moment to catch her breath, but to her dismay the professor was not at his desk. Snatching one of the sticky pads off his desk. The note was hurried, even a little vague, but she had no time for details. *Five o'clock, in my office, come alone.*

It was 5:15 PM when Stan waltzed through her door. "Always fashionably late, aren't you?" she grumbled from behind her desk.

"Settle down, killer," he replied with a smirk. "I had a lecture run a little late."

Barbara's expression softened. "I'm sorry about snapping it's just that I need you to take a look at this." She slid the journal and translation across her desk.

With a quizzical expression he opened the journal and ran his fingers across the pages. "Interesting," he mused. He picked up the translation, sat across from Barbara and took a pair of reading glasses from his shirt pocket.

I am writing this journal from our campsite at Dasamongueponke. My people and I have returned to Croatoan Island after investigating the events at Roanoke Island. I have lost track of time as a result of things which have taken place but I know the year to be 1590. Even as I am writing this, my mind still cannot comprehend the events that have happened on Roanoke Island. I awoke this morning as the early morning sun rose and I prepared supplies to trade with the settlers on the island. This has been a daily routine for me as I wished to learn more of the settlers' Christian religion. They have given me cultural artifacts from their lands in return of promises of protection from hostile tribes. I gathered the day's supplies and placed them in the boat and set sail for the colonists. As the boat touched the shore of the island I heard an unholy scream coming from the settler's camp. Our tribal weapons were primitive compared to the settlers and the only weapon I had on board was a spear with a crude iron tip. I grabbed it and ran for the colony. As I approached the tree line surrounding the settlement, I decided to climb a nearby tree to allow myself a view of the entire camp. I needed to be cautious due to recent attacks from the Powhatan tribes. As I gathered myself upon the tree, I was able to view the entire colony. When I looked down I witnessed the source of the scream and my blood turned to ice. There was an English woman whose age could not be determined as her face was covered in blood. She was being held by a tall, gaunt, ghostly figure with long claws and eyes of blood, who feasted on her flesh. I remained as still as night, as to not alert this creature of my presence, when all of a sudden he turned his demonic gaze in my direction. As the sun was my witness he embraced the woman and disappeared before my eyes, taking the woman with it.

16

I am unsure how long I sat, frozen upon my perch, waiting for the return of this foul creature. I hoped to see other colonists emerge from hiding, but none ever came. As my eyes surveyed the settlement I could see no movement or life from the small fort they had erected nor from any of their homes. My eyes strained against the daylight in an effort to catch even the slightest movement from the camp. My ears, long attuned to the sounds of the forest, sought to listen for any noise which would return normalcy to what I had just witnessed. Not a single sound could be heard, not the screech of a hawk nor even a deer prancing through the wood. All there was stood an empty camp.

After a long time had passed and I determined the area safe, I jumped from the tree and dropped my spear in my haste to return to my people. Upon my return, I told them of the creature at the English settlement. Achak, our tribal shaman explained that what I had seen was a Wendigo, a demonic spirit who was once a man but morphed into a hideous creature through acts of cannibalism. He told me it was possible the colonists turned to cannibalism as a result of the recent drought and inadvertently summoned this demonic entity. He advised me to gather some of our noblest warriors and accompany him to the island. With great haste we sailed to Roanoke and made our way to the settlement. Once there, we constructed a great fire and when we were finished Achak instructed us to form a large circle around the fire. He drew ancient Algonquin symbols into the dirt and chanted while dancing around the fire. Eventually his gaze turned toward the sky and a great sweat broke out upon his brow.

He danced for what seemed like ages until he stopped suddenly and turned his attention toward the forest. His gaze was locked onto the forest for several moments before he turned to me. The ritual was complete. According to Achak, the Wendigo was now banished from the area by the power of our ancestors. He approached a nearby tree along the border of the forest and tore the bark free. Using the tip of a spear he carved a single word into a tree: **CROATOAN**. I asked him the significance of the word. Achak looked at me through distant eyes and explained that the word signifies a Croatoan ritual of banishment had been performed and the Wendigo was no longer welcome here.

Achak commanded us to take down the houses and load them into our boats. At the time he said we could use materials from the houses to fortify our camp but later he admitted the haunted spirits of the colonists may be tempted to return to their homes if they had remained. As we returned to our camp, I could not help but think about my friend, John White, who befriended me and taught me his culture. I *pray for the souls of Roanoke Island and whoever will read this journal. I will place this book into the chest I received as a gift from John White, as I know that would be what he wanted. I hope the chest can withstand nature as well as time and that it reaches other English settlers. I pray they heed the words contained within. Roanoke Island may be cleansed now, but be wary that the demon who took the colonists away from these lands is only temporarily gone. May God protect future settlers to the island.*

   -Manteo 1589

Stan slowly removed his glasses and placed them on top of the translation. "Barbara, you are much better than me at identifying cultural artifacts. Are you positive this book is legitimate and not some sort of hoax? After reading this Loch Ness and Bigfoot come to mind. I am familiar with the history of Roanoke and of Manteo but I have never read of anything like this."

"Stan, you have known me a long time. I have spent hours researching the statements contained in that book. I am a hundred percent certain the chest and the book are authentic," she said firmly. "But what do you make of the writing and the timeline? Can it be real?" She noticed she had been wringing her hands like some kind of mythical witch about to boil children in her cauldron and ceased immediately.

Stan put his glasses on and studied the pages for what seemed an eternity. "I can tell you with certainty that the description of events here matches historical documents obtained from the voyages between and England and Roanoke Island. It matches up with documents obtained from the Jamestown colony's investigation into the Roanoke disappearance. Historically, Manteo was a representative of the Algonquins on Croatoan Island, was friendly to the colonists, learned English and eventually even converted to Christianity. If what is in this book is true then this would explain the disappearance of the Roanoke Island settlers which would be bigger than either what you or I can say on the subject. The best course of action would be to take these items to the Dean of Students and get his input on what we should do next."

Barbara relaxed a little. "Fine, I will meet up with you in the morning and we will head there together. Do you have a safe place to keep these items?"

Stan nodded. He returned the book to the chest, closed it and placed it into a cabinet underneath his desk. "I will see you tomorrow, right?" he asked.

Barbara nodded and they marched together toward the exit. The paused when they reached the Dean's office. The office was empty because the Dean was conducting a meeting across campus but the television he kept in his office was on. It was tuned to the local news station.

"*We have a breaking news bulletin from our local affiliate WSB-TV Atlanta,*" the anchorman announced. "*Initial reports are surfacing of a boat accident near Hatteras Island. Preliminary reports state a coast guard cutter received a distress call from the 'SS Zephyr', a fishing trawler based out of Norfolk, Virginia. A spokesman for the U.S. Coast Guard stated the trawler was empty when discovered. Statements from a spokesperson at the time....oh wait, what? Okay I have just been informed we are going to switch live to our station correspondent, Sean Stevens who is live at the scene.*"

"Hold on Stan, let's listen to this." She pulled him through the Dean's door and watched as Sean Stevens came on.

"*Thanks Bob. Hello folks, this is Sean Stevens reporting live from the coast of Hatteras Island. I have just been told by a representative within the Coast Guard that it has been confirmed the Zephyr had no crew aboard when discovered. I have with me live Captain Tom Benson of the U.S Coast Guard with some more information on the accident.*"

"*Thank you Sean. As of right now we have no information on the whereabouts of the crew. All life vests were secured on the ship and the navigational equipment along with the GPS seem to be in working order. We have technicians working on the devices to see if they can discover anything. Below deck, everything appears to be in order and there are no signs of distress or damage. From what we can see the boat is fully functional with no abnormalities in equipment. There was no food or water aboard, and signs suggest the craft was adrift for some time. All flares were present and the radio was in working order. The only thing we discovered was a word carved into a chair on the bridge next to some unidentified scratch marks in the steering controls.*"

"*What word was it, Captain,*" Stevens asked.

"*Well, the word was 'Croatoan'. As of right now we are not sure what it means. We are investigating to see if it may have been another vessel in the area at the time. We have conducted a perimeter search of the area in hopes of finding–*"

The rest of the news story evaporated as Barbara took a step toward the door. With her hand covering her mouth she looked at Stan in horror.

"Croatoan," Stan echoed the word as he continued to stare at the TV, wide-eyed. His hands opened and closed quickly, as if he they suddenly became numb and he was trying to restore blood circulation.

When he turned to her, a look of horror passed between them. He didn't need to say anything for she knew what he was thinking. The protection of the island was no more. That which was banished had returned. The word escaped her lips before she even realized she had uttered it.

Wendigo.

About the Author
Craig Gaydas

Even though I began my journey of writing at a late age, my desire to build worlds and create characters started at a very young age. 10 to be exact. I enjoyed world building games such as Dungeons and Dragons as well as immersing myself into superhero back stories via the "Marvel Universe" compendiums. I signed on with independent publishing house Creativia in early 2014 and haven't looked back.

Books by Craig Gaydas:

The Cartographer
The Cartographer 2: Reborn
The Cartographer 3: Timeless
Vendetta
The Last Hero
The Guardian Chronicles

River of Love

Eve Gaal

The guys at work called Lopez a schmuck. They used foul language to describe him, simply because he didn't drink. They also called him a flake because he didn't go to parties and wouldn't chum up to everyone at happy hour. They also speculated about his personal peccadilloes. Either he had a secret drug habit, or they figured he wasn't straight. They imagined him as a crossdressing loner who spent weekends trying on extra-large women's lingerie, after which he'd drown his sorrows with a mail-ordered craft beer kit. As if any of that mattered to how he did his job. Sometimes they took their assumptions too far, because none of the creative allegations were true. At office meetings, they locked him out if he was a minute late or blamed him if the copier broke. Small inconsequential things that actually made Al Lopez laugh, because deep inside he possessed a timid, but well-rounded sense of humor. He also didn't give a hamster's behind what the guys at work thought about his non-existent sex life.

A college diploma didn't help. Lopez had an air about him that made him seem regal. He had goals—both personal and work-related—all of which he ticked off in his head like a shopping list—each morning. On top of the achievement list or leader board, he maintained his quotas, staying self-motivated, aiming to inspire others with a spring in his step. How could this shy, determined fellow constantly be churning out so much success? The men in the office were bitter fools, jealous of his inner glow and yet, they seemed almost petty about all of it, as if their jealousy had more to do with his elegant suits, buffed up shoes and excellent head of hair. Lopez felt he was a humble man with gallons of faith and a heritage imbued with the promises and prayers of his ancestors, going back hundreds, perhaps thousands of years. Solid, unshakable and firm like a rock. Too bad the only person he shared his life with was his sweet, adoring sister, Bonnie.

The phone in Lopez's pocket vibrated during a meeting. He looked at the message and deleted it. Someone he didn't recognize had text messaged him about a meeting at midnight. Strange and vague, it sounded ominous. "Midnight on the bridge," it said. "Come alone." During a lull in the business meeting, he thought about the message and wondered about the bridge. He also wondered why they would want him to come alone. *Probably the office morons playing another joke,* he thought. He shook it off as a wrong number and closed another deal that day. At six, he descended the stairs and climbed into his luxury car to head home. Raindrops on his windshield reminded him a storm had moved through the city.

At the first traffic light, his phone vibrated but he didn't pick up the message. It had to be his sister wanting to know why he was late. The two of them were teaming up as good Samaritans in what was, in all honesty, a passive search for love and marriage. They were going to a church-function where they both volunteered, helping the homeless. The implausible idea consisted of the mere possibility that mingling with other do-gooders, might somehow spark interest in someone of the opposite sex. That was the hidden agenda and his calculated plan anyway, but after six months with nothing more than some matronly smiles, he wondered if they should change their approach. Sadly, they didn't like dancing or bars either, which left clubbing out of the picture too. His latest brainstorm centered on a much-anticipated vacation. Bathing suits, sand, sunshine and waves might be the perfect setting for romance. At least that's what it looked like in the travel brochures.

Typically punctual, a last-minute conference call with an aggravating European investor had made him late. He mumbled a short prayer, hoping his baby sister wouldn't be too upset. At the parking garage, he looked at his phone. "Midnight on the bridge," it said again. "Come alone." The clock in his sedan said one minute after seven and by midnight, he hoped to be dreaming of the upcoming Hawaiian vacation. Something made him answer the message, "Why?" When he didn't receive an immediate reply, he got out and locked the car before riding the elevator up to the two-bedroom apartment he shared with Bonnie.

"Hello? Anyone home?" he yelled, stepping into the kitchen. Silence. He moved into the bedroom and removed his necktie. "Bonnie?" The worst thing about serving at the food pantry was the plastic caps they had to wear—made him look like a geek. He dialed his sister's cell and she didn't answer. He turned on more lights. Glad to be home, he thought about the busy soup kitchen that fills up fast and stays busy until ten. He was worn-out anyway and heard rain hitting the windows, making this the perfect evening to stay home.

After a light dinner and a short workout lifting weights, Lopez relaxed in front of the television in plaid pajamas. He dozed off and began to dream about the mysterious message. The dream took him to the bridge in Seneca Falls or rather Bedford falls, where George Bailey was about to jump into the frigid ocean. "Don't do it George," he yelled, before Clarence even arrived. Lopez woke in a sweat. He looked at his Omega watch that glowed in the dark. It showed eleven minutes after eleven. He looked around and pulled himself into a sitting position. "Bonnie?" He went to her room and pushed open the door where a nicely made bed with a white coverlet and a lavender teddy bear waited for his sister to come home. *She should be here by now,* he thought, grabbing his coat and dialing her number at the same time.

Keys, keys. He jerked his head toward the kitchen, grabbed them and stormed down to his car in order to rush over to the pantry and find his sister. Still no answer but the five notices left by an unknown number still illuminated his message center on his phone. Could the messages be from Bonnie? Nah, it wasn't her number. Exiting the garage, rain hammered his car and he turned on the windshield wipers. Lopez grated his teeth. He figured he'd find out what all the fuss is about by stopping on that bridge on the way home. He prayed again, this time a long personal prayer and then the Lord's Prayer. He asked for forgiveness for being late and working too hard; even for acting smug in front of those who made fun of him at work. He turned on the window defroster to clear up the moisture and made a right turn towards the church where the familiar hall sat in the dark—no parishioners, no homeless and no volunteers. His tires screeched as he entered the large parking lot and looked around. No one—but he had to make sure. By this time, he thought he should call the police, but he reminded himself that his sister was a grown woman who had also finished college. His own co-dependent behavior toward his sibling drove him nuts.

Rain still pelted the town. He pulled up his collar, stepping into a puddle as he exited the vehicle. His phone had a built-in flashlight and he turned it on. Walking around to the back of the building, he noticed empty boxes shielding a few of the homeless who were trying to sleep. Lopez shined his flashlight onto a fellow with a long white beard. "Sorry to bother you but have you seen a lady in her mid-twenties around here?" Between the flannel pajamas, his wool coat and the sincere anxiety he felt about his sister, he felt his temperature rising. Perspiration tickled his neck, dripping down his back.

The old man rubbed his eyes, slowly pulling himself out of the box into the wet weather, "No, only Bonnie. She gave me this fine box. Don't you think it's wonderful?"

"Yes, yes, Bonnie," he practically spit the words into the wet evening. "She's my sister," he sighed with relief. "Where is she?" Relieved, Lopez followed the man's crooked finger and noticed his sister sitting on a bench with another man. They were holding hands under a large tree that somewhat shielded them from the deluge. Both of them were wearing the ugly, elasticized plastic caps. He approached, holding the flashlight. "Bonnie, it's me." He wiped moisture from his forehead. "Why are you still here?"

She rolled her eyes. "I'm here because Dan said he'd take me home. Sorry Al, but my cell phone is dead; forgot to charge it."

Dan? Who was Dan? Lopez inhaled and tried cooling down, quietly thanking his guardian angel. "You had me worried." He looked at the burly looking man in the blue shower cap. A large bushy moustache hid most of his face. His worn jacket had a logo encircled with embroidered flames.

Dan stood and shook his hand. "Think I remember you from last time. I've volunteered here for ten years. Name's Dan. I'm a retired fire captain. Think I'm in love with your sister. She's a beauty, even with that funny looking cap."

Bonnie blushed and Lopez shook Dan's hand. "Yes, I've seen you around, nice to finally meet you. So, you're giving her a ride?"

Dan turned around and went back to Bonnie. He hugged her tight. "We were thinking of going to the diner for pie and coffee. You're welcome to come."

"Nope, I'll pass but thanks—early meeting tomorrow." He walked over to his sister and gave her a quick, brotherly hug. "You'll be okay, right?" He whispered in her ear.

She smiled and nodded. "Love you Bro. Sorry."

Lopez went to his car. Both the rain and his heart seemed lighter now. Love? His heart pounded, racing gleefully inside his chest. Who would have thought that finally, after months of volunteer work, his sister would finally make a connection? When he turned out of the parking lot, he looked at the dashboard clock. It said five minutes until midnight. He drove in the direction of the bridge.

Water dripped from his nose. He was thrilled. The warmth in his soul radiated throughout his car, making the windows steam up on the inside. "Glory-be and hallelujah," he chanted several times while drumming on the steering wheel and "Thank you Almighty God!"

The traffic on the bridge consisted of two or three cars. This wasn't a large bridge, just an old ornate bridge with decorative motifs and historical significance. Somewhere in the middle of crossing over Schoharie Creek, while singing along to a gospel CD, his car moved in an unlikely direction and he lost control. As the bridge toppled, his fancy car tumbled into the swirling darkness below. The cold water engulfed the car before Lopez could roll down a window or open a door. If someone hadn't seen him sink, he was sure to die.

Out the back window, he could just see two cars hanging precariously on the side of a gap held together by ancient rebar, poking like stubble from old wet concrete. He thought he could see several dark shapes jump into the moving water that churned towards the Mohawk River. The muted sounds of sirens told him help was coming while Lopez frantically worked on unbuckling his seatbelt.

The rear window broke, and water rushed into the car, engulfing Lopez. He took a deep breath and held it, but didn't know what would happen. And though he didn't panic, the end looked near. *Help me God*, he thought, as he moved into the backseat towards the gushing water. He felt hands pulling him to safety. Water everywhere—a type of baptismal—the Living Water–Lopez closed his eyes and numbly floated away. Seconds later, air pushed inward and his lungs filled. He came to with someone giving him mouth-to-mouth necessitation. Water poured from his nose and his mouth. He gurgled, gulped and opened his eyes. *Was that Dan hovering over him on the shore?* Paramedics moved him to a a stretcher. Minutes later, he was in the ER where a lovely nurse held his hand. He blinked several times and smiled. "Hello," he said bashfully. "The entire bridge went out from under me."

"So, I heard. Glad you made it," she replied with a tone that sounded almost sarcastic. "Your sister's here with my brother." The nurse tended to his scratches with ointments and bandages. "Doesn't look like you broke any bones—can you move your big toe for me?"

"Huh?" He wiggled his toes and she smiled a wry smile.

"Bonnie's your sister, right?"

"She's here?"

"Yes, she's here with Dan. Dan's my brother. He's the one who saved you."
She spoke slowly as if maybe he had lost his marbles in the bottom of the
murky river.

This angel in a uniform stood over him smiling and talking to him as if he
fell out of a special- needs bus. "Dan's your brother? You don't look anything
like him." Lopez looked at her tender lashes and pink lips. His eyes traveled to
her nametag that said Patty.

She laughed. "Yeah, he has a lot more facial hair. I think you'll be going
home with them soon."

Bonnie ran in and embraced her brother. "Al," she shouted, obviously out of
breath. Dan was steps behind her trying to keep up, but his clothes were wet,
and he moved slowly, shivering and uncomfortably. A towel wrapped around
his broad shoulders. "Oh my goodness, what a miracle—I kept asking Dan about
you and he wasn't sure what to tell me." Tears rolled down her cheeks. "Why
did you go on the bridge? I thought you were going back to our place?"

"He'll be fine." Patty reached over towards Bonnie and caressed her back.
"Let me go get the doctor so he *can* go home."

"Hey buddy," Dan grinned at the man lying on the gurney. "Lucky we were
headed in that direction. What a fluke. No one died, and you are the only injured
party. That bridge has withstood everything for a hundred years. Storms, hail,
heavy snow, floods, marches, parades and then all of a sudden-swoosh. Just
like that it crumbles to pieces." He shook his head in disbelief. "So weird, but
sure glad you're going to be okay. Few more seconds and you would have had
hypothermia."

"Or drowned?" Bonnie wailed.

Patty returned with more towels for her brother. "Dan, you're making a
mess."

"So what else is new? Sisters—they never let you forget your shortcomings."

Lopez looked into Dan's rough-hewn face. *Who was this man of men?* He
looked over at Bonnie who continued weeping tears of joy. "Bonnie, stop
crying." He watched Patty wiping up mud behind her brother. He wondered
whether Patty was married but didn't think he could be bold enough to ask.
His mind raced at the possibilities when he considered that these two might
also be a similar set of codependent siblings. A few seconds later, Patty came
to his side with questions about how he was feeling.

"I'm supposed to check your vitals and then report back to Doc. Take a deep breath."

He inhaled and looked at her latex gloved hands. No ring seemed to be a good sign, but nurses in the ER kept jewelry to a minimum. "Your lungs are clear." She felt his pulse. "Little bit of rapid heartbeat but after what you've been through tonight, I'm not surprised." Next, she took his temperature. "Perfect."

"Perfect? Me? Never, but I try." He looked at Dan trying to cheer up his sobbing sister and thanked the heavens and the legions of seraphim, cherubim and all the saints above for sending protection during this freak accident. Suddenly, while staring into Patty's sparkling eyes, he realized it wasn't an accident at all. *He thought of his cell phone sitting on the bottom of a rushing creek and the message to go to the bridge at midnight. Who sent the messages he wondered? How did they know?*

Go ahead you dummy, he told himself. Voices in his head told him that being shy never helped anyone reach his or her ultimate goals. *Go for it. You almost died, moron. Take a chance. Life is short. Do it. Ask and don't turn back.* "You, however, look perfect to me. Are you single or married?"

Crimson circles formed in the middle of Patty's cheeks. "I'm referring to your temperature, Mr. Lopez," she answered in a serious and professional tone. "Single." She pursed her lovely lips, tilted her head and looked over at Dan who winked.

Lopez smiled, springing to a sitting position in the bed. "Dan, can we go get that slice of pie at the diner now?" Bonnie and Patty giggled like conspiring sisters. "I have this story I want to tell all of you, but you'd never believe me anyway."

Dan stood up and dropped one of the towels onto a chair. "Oh yeah—sounds like a challenge–bet I've heard it."

"Well sorry, I can't go right now. Anyone notice I'm still working here?" Patty had both hands on her hips. Making a face at Dan, she moved one hand to pick up the wet towel from the chair, as if it was a dead weasel. "Guess I'll have to hear the story later."

Lopez put his legs on the ground and found his coat and shoes in a white bag. "Oh no—not going to happen. This is a story for all of us and you have to listen to it from beginning to end. Either that or I have to stay here and be your patient for the rest of my life."

Patty grinned and handed Lopez the rest of his belongings, including his waterproof watch. She pointed to the clock on the wall. "It's three o'clock in the morning and that diner probably ran out of pie anyway. Go ahead and stay."

"Well suit yourself Sis, Bonnie and I are going to the diner. See-ya later." Dan pulled Bonnie out into the corridor leaving Lopez to fend for himself.

"Your brother's cool," he said, noticing his confidence level seemed to have taken a nosedive off a shallow ridge.

"He's something else that's for sure–saves more cats in trees than PETA."

"That's nice. I was like a drowning cat and he saved me too." He rubbed his neck. "Guess I'll have to postpone my vacation because my neck muscles feel sore. Good thing I bought the cancellation insurance."

"Here, have some aspirin." She held out a plastic cup of water and put two capsules into his hand. Staying busy, she put instruments into drawers while she spoke. "So, what's this story you want to tell us that we won't believe? Does it have to do with falling off of a bridge in the middle of the night?"

"It does. But if I told you the rest of it, I'd have to close the door and maybe…well, I'm not very good at these types of things." Now his cheeks burned, and he felt dizzy from the earlier ordeal, so he sat back down on the side of the bed, and rubbed his neck again.

"Maybe I can help." She drew the curtain around the bed and closed the door. When she came back, she took hold of his bandaged hand. "Now you can tell me."

He leaned forward, inhaling her sweet perfume and whispered into her ear. "I can't because it's a miracle."

"What?"

"You know." He looked down at the vinyl floor and felt embarrassed.

She closed her eyes and pulled him close. "Just one kiss and you can tell me the story tomorrow after work," she whispered, as soft pink lips graced his cheek and moved towards his mouth. "That's if you don't fall into anymore rivers. I can't guarantee my brother will be there."

Lopez nodded, passionately returning her kiss while holding her hands. His heart skipped a beat and he felt as if a tide had floated him out to sea like driftwood. He remembered that the Mohawk word for driftwood is Schoharie. Al's heart now gone—past the bridge—completely–utterly–captivated–by an angel named Patty. "You smell like the river," she purred with a smile and a make-believe growl. "And I like it."

30

Two embracing hearts floated like driftwood for several months, in a marine layered fog until landing on a sun-drenched beach with a strip of white sand, swaying palms, on the island of Hawaii. There, they met up with two more bobbing hearts, Dan and Bonnie. All four of them were married, and now both couples live happily ever after. The guys at work think of Lopez as a hero. Gorgeous wife—almost drowned—respect. They don't tease him, bully him and never, ever call him a schmuck anymore.

About the Author
Eve Gaal

Eve Gaal, M.A. is the author of the romantic novel Penniless Hearts and a faith-based, fantasy novella titled The Fifth Commandment. Her freelance creative writing business is: **Desert Rocks** and her inspirational blog: **Intangible Hearts**. Find links to her stories and poems at http://www.evegaal.com/. Her work has also appeared in *The Los Angeles Times* and *Datebook, a weekend edition of The **Daily Pilot.*** A precocious child, her dad told her to write about anything and everything, even making sure she had a toy typewriter by age four. Born in Boston, but a longtime Californian, she lives with her husband and two mischievous Chihuahuas.

Books by Eve Gaal:

The Fifth Commandment
Penniless Hearts

Links:

Website: http://www.evegaal.com/

Ayn Rand

Kenna McKinnon

Danger, luv, your fingers will suffer!

Reggie Donovan was Mary's first supervisor in the coveted entry level job as a junior clerk-typist at Ohio Standard Oil & Gas Co. The year was 1963. Eighteen-year-old Mary Henderson sat erect at a small desk in front of a re-conditioned Remington manual office typewriter. The typewriter was broken. She didn't know what to do. Mr. Donovan slouched at his huge desk in the office at the end of the hall, his door ajar, so she could see the cabinet beside him with the extra paper she needed to roll into the maw of the typewriter. He would try to slam her fingers in the drawer before she could withdraw her hand. He had done it many times before. She was afraid. She was afraid to tell him that the old Remington refused to strike the keys onto the black and red striped fabric ribbon, as it had so faithfully for the past ten months since she started the entry level job. He would tell her to fix it herself.

He did.

"Fix it yourself, Sweetlips," Reggie sneered. "We're behind budget already. If you're too incompetent to manage your machine then we'll have to put you to work down the hall at the files. You know what that means. Demotion!"

He threw open the drawer beside him, and dared her with his eyes to put her hand in there to extract the needed tool, the coveted typing paper, and most of all, the manual that would tell her how to fix the stubborn keys.

Mary set her lips in a tight line and her hand darted into the cavernous drawer, snatched the screwdriver, the paper, and the manual, then darted out again, just as Mr. Donovan slammed the drawer, almost catching her hand in it. John Austin, one of the bookkeepers from the general office down the hall, happened into the room just at that point. Mary ducked her head and flushed with the rush of emotions. She noticed his bulging biceps strained at the fabric of his white shirt. John frowned and ran a hand through his curly brown hair, his eyes bright blue with anger.

"You tried to catch her hand in the drawer," he accused. Reggie glanced down and the corners of his mouth stretched out but no humor showed in his eyes. His face was brick red.

She skittered out of the room.

John Austin followed her after a bit, and took the tool from her hand. He opened the manual to the appropriate page. Frowning again, he set to work.

"I don't know what's the matter with him," he said. "This company is so cheap that yes, they expect you to fix your own machine."

"It's okay," Mary whispered. She blushed.

"How's your hand, dear?"

"It's fine. He missed my hand."

"Does he do that a lot?"

"He does that every time I come in there. He wants me to get something out of the drawer then he tries to slam it on my hand."

"Hmmmm." John turned the roller and snapped the keys so they hummed. "We have a union, you know."

"I don't want to make any trouble."

"How old are you?"

"Eighteen."

"This your first job?" John's hypnotic blue eyes smiled down at her.

"Yes. I thought I was lucky to get it. My mother told me I was lucky and that I shouldn't be like one of those ugly feminists and try to be boss over a man. My mother told me this was a good job for me. I guess she was right."

"There are lots of jobs available, dear. Though, we don't want to lose you. You're sweet, and a good worker. Very quiet, aren't you? Don't give Mary a compliment, they say in the office, she'll blush and go even quieter than usual. You live at home, Mary?"

"No, I moved out a year ago. My parents live in Grande Prairie."

"That's five hundred miles north. Why'd you move here to Calgary?"

"I had a baby," she whispered.

"Oh." He frowned. A great disgrace in 1963. Parents had thrown her out with twenty dollars in her pocket and told her to seek out the Salvation Army home for unwed mothers here in Calgary. It was very hush-hush in Grande Prairie. Some parents were more compassionate than others. But Mary figured that her parents weren't that type.

"What happened to the baby?" he asked.

"I gave him up for adoption."

Of course, typical for the time. Poor little thing, barely a baby herself, she had to grow up fast. She knew she didn't deserve this. But he could see why she was desperate to keep the job. The senior Mrs. Henderson's terror of feminism obviously was ill founded for her meek and quiet daughter. He smiled.

He rejoined his co-workers at their desks in the middle of the room, all dressed in almost identical dark suits, white shirts, and ties. Their fingers were smudged with ink as they bent over their binders to figure, transcribe, and eventually collate hundreds of reports that had been run off on the Gestetner machine operated by the ink-spattered Millie in the back room. At precisely ten a.m. every morning a bell would ring, and they would all surge toward the coffee room for twenty minutes of camaraderie. Mary sat silent, sipping on her cup of coffee and a New Yorker pastry from the cart that came around twice a day from the cafeteria downstairs.

The shy clerk-typist went home every night to an attic apartment which she shared with another unwed mother she'd met at the Salvation Army. Both girls were thin. They didn't eat well. Marianne Pecoski and Mary Henderson, an unlikely couple to be friends but out of necessity sought one another's companionship and a shared financial responsibility. Both dated now, Marianne a young corporal named Marcus James, in the Princess Patricia's Canadian Light Infantry, deployed for its second rotation in 1963, and Mary Henderson with a draftsman, Robert Scott, whom she'd met through Marcus. They often double dated. Marianne married first, leaving Mary with the run of the attic, which she decorated with orange tablecloths and batik prints. Her boyfriend, Robert, bought her a small Zenith black and white television set, which her cantankerous German landlord demanded not be set up in the bedroom, so it was put in a corner alcove under the sloping roof. The alcove was the only other area of the apartment with enough room.

Robert also bought her a hairdryer, so he wouldn't have to wait interminable hours for her hair to dry in rollers on a Saturday afternoon before they went out.

She cooked him fried chicken – browned it for fifteen minutes then served it. He advised her that he didn't care for chicken but ate it, pink and glossy through his white teeth.

Grateful, Mary gushed, "I love you." In her heart, she wasn't sure. She was so young, and so cheated of life. She yearned for her baby. Robert understood, and she was grateful for that, too.

The attic owned a clunky old black telephone that hung on the wall. Her number was TE 1-6403. The phone was a rotary dial, of course, and she had to go through an operator on the rare occasion she called her parents long-distance. Mary's voice was often raspy as she was so shy, and unused to talking or being courteously heard, more particularly on that unfamiliar instrument which rarely rang.

Robert would call her, but more often came right over or picked her up after work in his little red Austin Healey Sprite, but they were together every night in any case. He lived with his aunt, who had a modern turquoise color touch tone phone.

The telephone was important tonight, because Robert had not shown up, and someone else called. The bookkeeper's voice was husky. "Mary, this is John from work. I hope you don't mind. I got your number from the personnel files in Donovan's office. He leaves them unlocked." The message was ominous, if a little vague in the details. "Midnight, on the bridge. Come alone."

John Austin could mean only one bridge, the Centre Street Bridge with the stone lions at each end, perched so high that many busy drivers and pedestrians didn't realize they were there. Mary's apartment was downtown, close to Centre Street and the bridge. An acquaintance had sworn the lions followed her home at night, and hid in her closet, their large yellow eyes glowing in the dark. Mary shivered. She considered calling Robert but he lived with his aunt, and she was a jealous and interfering woman who would worm out of her nephew the reason for the call, and certainly persuade him that Mary should handle this on her own, or worse, that Mary was not to be trusted.

She envied other people their fluid conversations. She could not bring herself to that rapt exchange which good friends ought to enjoy. Robert liked her that way. He had searched for many years for a girl who would keep her fucking mouth shut.

She thought now of Robert and wondered where he'd gone, and she thought of John Austin and the cryptic phone call. She had no idea why the bookkeeper would be interested in such a meeting, nor if this was some kind of hoax. Mary, trained to be obedient of authority, followed her nose to what might prove to be an interesting mystery that might solve all her problems at work with the cruel Reggie Donovan. She felt that John Austin was her champion at work. Otherwise, she told herself, I am being foolish to venture out at midnight to the center of the city. She thought of John's curly brown hair and his mesmerizing eyes. Surely, he meant well. A rush of excitement coursed through her young blood.

Mary glanced at her mother's nursing watch, which she had worn since junior high school. It was ten thirty. The short walk to Centre Street Bridge would take her twenty minutes, at most. The area was well lit by streetlights and also there would be some traffic there, even at that time of night, as it was a major thoroughfare from downtown to the north part of the city. Mary kept a small flashlight in her cheap plastic purse. Her father had advised her to carry a knife, she remembered, but Robert said an attacker could overwhelm her defenses and use the knife against her. Together, Robert and her father would make the perfect man. Mary sighed. She hadn't been home since the baby was born. She wasn't welcome; they had been clear about that. Marianne and Robert were her only friends here, and maybe John now, but what could he want with her?

Sixty-five minutes ticked by. Mary gathered her coat around her, took her plastic purse and the flashlight, and left the house. She tottered on high heels along the dark streets, heels clacking and echoing in the fog shrouded October night. She was too innocent to be afraid at that moment, too used to walking alone in dangerous areas of the city, too used to being on her own without help or protection, to be afraid at midnight in this familiar city.

When she got to the bridge she could see clearly through the fog from the Bow River below that a lone figure leaned against the balustrade on the south end, shrouded in an old topcoat and tweed cap. She drew closer, her breath ragged. Her heart fluttered and perspiration moistened her forehead, but with the bravado of the young, she called out, "Who's there?"

The tall young man with the curly brown hair and eyes like violets moved into the glow of a streetlamp. "It's me, John."

"What do you want?" She drew her tattered coat closer around her shoulders. A cool wind swirled the fog away and she could see him clearly.

"Thank you for coming, Mary. I'm sorry for the drama, but I had to talk to you, and it isn't right to visit a lady at her apartment this late at night, and especially a young lady who has a boyfriend looking out for her. I had to talk to you."

"Why the bridge?"

"It's well lit and close to my house. I knew you live in a house on Centre Street as well. I know it's late. I wanted to give you enough time to get ready. I know ladies don't like to be rushed. They spend a lot of time in the powder room before going out, that's what my sisters always did."

"I live in an attic in a big old house downtown, above the landlords. I have a roommate. She knows where I am," she lied.

He was standing in front of her, his hands outstretched, a smile on his face that crinkled the corners of his eyes. The front of his topcoat was unbuttoned, and she could see the muscles flexing beneath his chest as he leaned toward her. "You're safe with me. Let's walk somewhere warmer."

"At this time of night?" Mary wished she'd worn more sensible shoes. "There's nothing open."

"Robin Donuts is just around the corner. They're open all night. I often go there."

"Do you live near here?" she asked.

"Just on the other side of the bridge."

She considered this. "You don't sleep much, do you?"

"I wanted to warn you. Don't go to work tomorrow."

She considered this, too. Images of the cruel Reggie Donovan cascaded through her mind. Maybe he'd finally fallen off the turnip truck, as Robert would have said.

"Uhhhhh…"

They walked along the side of the road, facing traffic. Occasionally a semi rumbled past or a late-night insomniac hurried by, head huddled against the cruel wind.

"I don't know why you asked me to come alone."

He didn't answer, but reached out and took her slim white hand in his sturdy fingers. "I have a better job offer for you, Mary. You mustn't come to work in the morning and face Reggie and his bullying. I can't stand it."

"What job?"

The cheerful red and white doors of Robin Donuts loomed through the misty night. He opened the door for Mary and both entered. The boy behind the counter smiled at them as they entered. He placed a large tray of donuts on the rack behind him. They could see another assistant in the back of the store, behind large plate glass windows, preparing donuts for the next day's morning rush.

"Two coffees," John said, then lifted an eyebrow. "Is that all right?"

"Okay."

He stirred sugar and cream into his and she sipped hers black. The boy behind the counter wiped his hands on his white apron and placed two jelly donuts in front of them, then returned to reading the late-night edition of the Calgary Herald. John and Mary sat in companionable silence.

"What's Reggie going to do to me tomorrow?"

"It's not what he's going to do tomorrow. It's how he treats you every day. I'm not going to stand for it. I've been looking around for another job, too, as a copywriter at the Herald. I spent two years as an English Major at the University of Calgary, then I dropped out to get a job. But I'm more than a bookkeeper, and that's not my passion. I submitted a couple pieces of good copy to the editor and he gave me an interview yesterday. He was very encouraging. They sat me down to write something for them, under pressure. I don't think he believed I wrote the copy I gave him, as my dad is a writer of some note."

"Did you do it?"

"Yeah, I came up with something that blew his socks off. So, he offered me the job. I'm going to give notice to Ohio Standard tomorrow."

"It'll be funny working there without you."

Bobby's Girl was playing on the jukebox. The boy behind the counter threw a quarter in Mary's direction and grinned, meaning she should make her four selections, but she was too shy to get up and do that, though John urged her to choose something. Finally, she gave the quarter back to the clerk behind the counter. They continued to sit on the red leather stools together, while the boy wandered over to the shining new Wurlitzer and punched the buttons to play the latest pop music from England.

"A new group you might like from Liverpool," he called over his shoulder. "They're called the Beatles." The jukebox clanked and *All My Loving* rang out, followed by *Baby It's You* and *Do You Want to Know a Secret*?

John grinned. "I've heard of them. Thanks."

"What do you mean, you have a job for me? I have a job."

"Not a good one and not a safe one. I'm surprised you didn't lose your fingers yesterday when Donovan slammed the drawer. He purposely tried to catch your hand. I don't want you working for a company that's so cheap you have to fix your own typewriter. Come with me to the Herald."

"This is so sudden."

"I didn't know until tonight that I got the job. Joe, the editor, called me at home around nine o'clock tonight. A paper never sleeps. I'd be working nights and so would you."

"I didn't get an interview."

"No, but I put a good word in for you and Joe said he'd try you out. They're looking for an entry level girl and seemed pretty interested. They know old Reggie at Ohio Standard, too. He knew what I meant when I told him you deserve something better. You'd be typing up classified ads at nights and taking ads over the phone. It pays a little better than Donovan pays, too. Would you consider it, Mary?"

"I don't know."

"Say yes." He leaned over her, his sparkling blue eyes holding hers. "You don't think it's a coincidence that I took rooms downtown so close to yours, do you? Or that I happened to come into Reggie's office just as you were in there?"

"Oh. I didn't think of that." She initially felt suffocated, but her heart lightened and the choking sensation in her throat lessened as the reality of what was happening struck her. This attractive man really liked her, and she didn't have to marry Robert out of desperation. John Austin stared into her eyes.

"I'm not used to somebody taking care of me," she whispered. The jelly donuts lay untouched.

Later, he walked her home and tried to kill her.

They stood together at the door to her house while she fumbled with the key. He moved so that he blocked her way and his eyes flashed with an explosion of something strange. Confused, Mary buried her head in his old wool topcoat and tried to make her way around his muscular form. He grasped her cruelly with both hands and she knew there would be bruises on her shoulders the next morning. If she survived.

"You little tramp, you deserve this. You're nothing but used goods. You owe me something. After all, I almost got you a job!"

She fought silently and fiercely. His hands closed around her windpipe. She thumped against the stout wooden door of the old house. The two of them didn't notice a light come on downstairs and two figures silhouetted against the glass.

The door burst open. Her landlord towered, a German behemoth, in his pajamas, with a baseball bat in his hand. "Dummkopf! Get away from her!" The man's wife stood behind her husband in the entryway that led upstairs to the attic rooms. She brandished a frying pan.

"Whore!" The bookkeeper threw Mary into the foyer and ran, but not before the German's wife, in her flannel nightgown, struck his head a good blow with the frying pan. Her husband smashed his retreating buttocks with the bat. Mary gasped and before her landlords could stop her, she grabbed a wrought iron fireplace poker from the umbrella stand and ran out into the night. All the pent-up rage in her spilled out – against her selfish and uncaring parents, the selfish father of her child, Robert who wanted a wife who would shut the fuck up, Reggie Donovan who tried to slam her hand in a drawer on purpose every day, and now John Austin, a man who had deceived and affronted her. She ran after him, crying and laughing at the same time, until she caught up to him on the bridge and a stone lion roared so loud in her head that she couldn't stand it and she ran John Austin through with the hook of the fireplace poker and then as he lay bleeding under the arch of the lower bridge, she ran him through again and again, with the tip of the sharp black wrought iron poker, and he was so surprised and so dazed by the blows from the frying pan and bat that he didn't and couldn't defend himself. After he was pierced through a dozen times she put her dainty size nine foot on the muscular thrust of his chest and he pulled her leg to him in a paroxysm of agony. A gaggle of pedestrians gathered to watch, mesmerized, as Mary fought her demons. The ululation of a police siren interrupted the bloody mess.

When the sheriffs arrived, they assessed the situation and informed Mary she had acted in self defense. Her landlords backed her up.

Robert had been drinking at the Electric Toby Lounge that night. Mary elucidated him the next day of the happenings at midnight on October 23, 1963. Marianne came back when she heard that Mary needed her. In 1963 there was little talk of feminism, but Mary felt her mother's worst fears had come true.

"I must be like Ayn Rand," she whispered, then cleared her throat and shouted it, free at last. Mary never whispered nor apologized again. "I'm Ayn Rand!"

About the Author
Kenna McKinnon

Kenna McKinnon is a Canadian freelance writer, author of *SpaceHive* (2012), and *Bigfoot Boy: Lost on Earth*, as well as *Benjamin and Rumblechum, The Insanity Machine; Blood Sister; Short Circuit and Other Geek Stories; DISCOVERY: A Collection of Poetry, Den of Dark Angels,* and *Engaging the Dragon.* Her most memorable years were spent at the University of Alberta, where she graduated with a degree in Anthropology. Kenna is a member of the Writers' Guild of Alberta and a professional member of the Canadian Authors Association. She has three wonderful children and three grandsons. Her hobbies include fitness, health, drawing, reading, walking, music, cooking and baking for friends.

Books by Kenna McKinnon:

Engaging the Dragon
SpaceHive
Benjamin & Rumblechum
Den of Dark Angels
Blood Sister
Short Circuit and Other Geek Stories
The Insanity Machine
Discovery: A Collection of Poetry

Links:

Author's blog: http://KennaMcKinnonAuthor.com
Facebook: https://www.facebook.com/KennaMcKinnonAuthor
Twitter: http://www.twitter.com/KennaMcKinnon
Goodreads: http://www.goodreads.com/author/dashboard
LinkedIn: http://www.linkedin.com/in/kennamckinnon

The Witching Hour

Mari Collier

Raven had always liked midnight. The time and the dark skies fitted her name and her disposition. Her hair was black as midnight and she kept it long and flowing. She would like to have her eyes just as dark, but at times they could be a yellowish color. Maybe contacts would solve that. That might solve one problem, but would create another.

It had started when she was a preteen and she and her friend would walk to the park after dinner. It was a small town and no one worried about them. They could meet friends and hang out. They no longer played tag over the bridge, but if one was delayed or didn't show, a note would be left under the small boulders and rocks used for landscaping at the bridge. If her friend left early, Raven could run for hours.

Later she walked in the park and over the bridge with her first boyfriend. She couldn't call him her boyfriend at home, but everyone at school knew. Sometimes they would arrange to meet there after one of his football games. One Halloween they met at the bridge at the witching hour before joining the others. She would sneak back there alone when the moon was full. Then her father was transferred and the park and bridge became a memory, but soft, star filled nights did not.

She loved to see the stars when they were not hidden behind the clouds that were a normal phenomenon in the Northwest. She often walked the road by her house at night, or the streets if she were in Seattle. The hours she spent at work and sleeping were cutting into her night roaming time.

"I need a new position," she announced to her lunch companion, Emma. They were in the company cafeteria, enjoying an organic steak salad. "One that doesn't involve so many hours."

Emma swallowed and looked up from her plate. "Where do you plan to find one like that in the software or electronics world? I don't know of any that have anything but ridiculous hours. It's why they pay so well. If someone hears you spouting that nonsense, they'll say it is because you are a woman and can't hack it."

Raven frowned. "I can compete with any of them. Why would they think that of me?"

Emma laughed. "Because you are a woman with long, black hair, and a figure most of us would die for."

Raven shrugged, but that answer didn't solve her problem. She knew part of it was a desire for privacy. Later she considered as she wandered down her lane and onto the road that went by her house and property. What if she were to start her own company? She could set her own hours then. That bubble burst immediately. She knew those that had done so. They worked even longer hours. Winning the lottery was such a distant chance, she didn't even consider it. At least her vacation started on Monday and then she could indulge in the night hours for three weeks. The first was at a live theatre production on Saturday and a party afterwards that she had promised to attend with Emma.

* * *

Raven walked with Emma to the party at the club two blocks away from the theatre. The crowd and the night swirled around them.

"Wasn't the woman who played Rose fantastic!" Emma enthused.

"Yes," answered Raven. She looked around at the crowd. None seemed aware of the black velvet being held at bay because of all the lights. Should she make her excuses and leave? It was too late they were crossing the street to the café and Emma was waving at someone.

"It's Candy and her group. Let's hurry." Emma tugged at her arm. "Quit looking upward when we have to cross a street. Jeez! You'll get yourself killed one of these times." One thing about Emma, she was never without a word for every occurrence.

She left the night and the brightly lit street and entered the café where some-one waved them to the back room. As they moved towards the back, a slender, dark haired man turned and smiled, as he lifted a glass of deep red wine.

"Hello, my name is Alex. What can I order for you to commemorate our meeting?" His smile was electric and his features seemed to remind her of a long ago acquaintance.

"Hello, I'm Raven and this is my friend, Emma." Raven smiled at him. Perhaps this wouldn't be a wasted evening. It was still one night before a full moon. "I'd like a nice merlot to celebrate."

He turned to the table and paid the bartender as he said, "The merlot."

He partially turned to look at her. "In the words of an old line when meeting a lovely female you've never met before, do you come here often?"

"No, I don't, and thank you," said Raven as he handed the glass to her. "I much prefer walking outside in the dark."

"Egad, a woman after my own heart. I'd ask you outside now, but that would mean leaving our drinks. Is there any place in this room less crowded?"

Emma was at the bar chatting with others that she knew or had just met. With Emma it was difficult to tell.

"Well, moving away from the bar would probably free up some room."

He grinned at her and pointed at a table near the back and they walked to it. "You look familiar," Raven said as they sat in the chairs. "Were you ever in a small city called Dunlap?"

"Not that I know of or remember. Why do you ask?"

"I used to live there and your features are similar to a boy I knew. His last name was White."

Alex grinned. "That leaves me out entirely. I'm Alex d'Argaton, by the way. Now it is your turn. Is Raven really your name?"

Raven laughed. She usually didn't explain, but this time she did. "My mother really wanted to be a hippie, but the movement had long been passé. She did pick one of the strange first names for me when I was born with a head of black hair. I became Raven Maria Devon."

Alex raised his glass to her. "It fits you. Now I do hope you tell me you live an exotic life to fulfill the name."

"Hardly, I work for a software company that requires all sorts of lengthy hours. Nine and ten hour days are common."

"Well, in that case you need the exercise of night walks. Would you like to take one now? You seem as interested in that wine as I am. We could share stories." He raised his dark eyebrows and grinned.

Raven considered. "It's hardly dark out there with all the street lights and I am not walking into some darkened alley in this city. It really wouldn't be safe."

"Nor would I ask that of you. This is a stroll of a couple of blocks to the park and a wonderful view from there."

"I found the view in parks limited to trees and playground equipment." She snapped and started to turn away.

"Ah, you have not been to Overpass Park then." She could hear the laughter in his voice.

"Well," she turned back. "No, I haven't. I saw some mention of it, but really paid no attention. Picnicking isn't my thing."

"In that case, may I offer my arm to escort you there?" He put down the wine, stood, gave a slight bow, and extended his elbow. There was something old fashioned and courtly in his movements and in his words. It was intriguing. Was he an actor? He was handsome enough.

Raven felt herself warming to this handsome, young man. She, would, of course, do a proper search tomorrow, but for tonight a walk to the park would be good. She could text Emma if she didn't return. Tonight with all the people everything was safe enough.

The night air was city air, laced with rubber and gas fumes. A haze seemed to circle the street lights, but there were crowds of people to ensure her safety. She would decide about the rest of the walk once they reached the park.

The traffic lights seemed to favor their progress as they changed each time they arrived and they marched up into the park pathway. It too was well lit and people strolled or sat on benches. The air seemed less acrid here and he led her to a bridge that arched up and over a manmade waterway before descending to the other side. Only one other couple stood at the top and they moved to walk down to the other side.

Raven and Alex stopped as they reached the middle of the bridge. He smiled and pointed upward. One could see a few stars peppering the black night and a pale almost full moon half hidden by clouds. Below they could see a few people moving in the half colors and darkening shadows. It was nearing midnight. Watch yourself, she thought. This is nearing the witching hour. Don't let yourself become bewitched.

"Well?" Alex asked.

Raven had to smile at him. "I'll admit that I would never have thought to walk up here at night, nor have I been to the park during the day. How did you discover this?"

Alex shrugged. "I spend a lot of night hours wandering." He looked at her. "Sometimes I visit at midnight just to see what it is like. If you don't care for this, would you consider going elsewhere with me?"

"Not tonight. I have to drive Emma home. Plus, I don't know you that well. Why don't we meet for coffee tomorrow afternoon?"

He flinched a bit at that question. "No," he said. "I'm sorry to be so abrupt. My day is planned. I am free later in the evening though. Where you would like to meet? The popular crowd bistro or another place?"

"I live over in Eldertown. How about the coffee shop called Joe's Coffee? It's right on the main street through town. You can't miss it."

"I'll be there as soon as it is dark." He lifted her hand and kissed it, turned and led her back down the way they had walked.

Once they were out on the crowded street, he smiled. "Tomorrow then," and melted away into the crowd.

Strange, Raven thought. How could he disappear so rapidly? She shrugged and went back into the café to look for Emma.

She spent the next day catching up on her laundry, shopping, and house cleaning. She was almost too tired to go to Joe's, but for some reason he had not offered his phone number and she had not offered hers either. She had checked Facebook and Googled his name. Nothing had come up on either. Was he from another country? Being from another country shouldn't prevent a name from appearing in the search. The next time she tried Bing. Then she tried just the surname on both Google and Bing with the same results. Still no match. She needed more information. You couldn't trust a stranger in today's world. Too many were trying cons and scams.

It was nine-ten p.m. when she drove into Joe's parking lot. Fall was almost here and night was coming earlier. That was another problem with the Pacific Northwest. The further north one lived the longer daylight lingered during Daylight Savings Time.

She didn't see Alex in the parking lot or in the seating area when she walked into the coffee shop. Hmm, she thought, I wonder if he'll be here. Raven ordered her latte, took the cup, and sat at a table in the back. She took out her cell phone to check messages and discovered about ten from work. She had ignored the phone all day. Why did they bother to message her during her vacation? Most were from Emma and filled with the usual chatter.

"You seem all involved." Alex stood there with cup in hand smiling at her. "You don't mind if I take this chair, do you?" He set the cup down and sat across from her. "Perfect place and not too busy."

"Not this time of night." She turned off the cell and put it away.

"I hope I didn't interrupt your perusal of one of the classics."

Raven smiled and picked up her cup. "No, just catching up on my text messages from friends and ignoring the email from work."

"I thought you were on vacation."

"I am, Alex. That is why I ignored them. I'll answer them in the morning. Maybe the people that sent them will have sense enough to go home and sleep if I don't answer until then."

Alex raised his eyebrows. "People don't sleep where you work or they just don't sleep at night?'

"It is a software company and we do tend to put in long hours." Raven shrugged. "It's why we have the perks that your old businesses would never have allowed in their corporate structure." She took a swallow from her cup.

"Ah, yes, the modern society. Is that why you live in such a small burg? To escape the horrors of autos, busses, planes, and an overwhelming abundance of people?"

"Partly, except I don't live within the town limits. I'm outside of them on an acreage where there isn't even a streetlight on the road. Now if I could convince my neighbors to dismantle or turn off their yard lights at night it would be perfect." She drank from her cup again as she eyed him.

"Ah, they want the light. Why did they move out there then?"

"I have no idea. Perhaps, they believe it will help keep them safe. Do you live out in the suburbs or right in the city?" She realized the question seemed to raise a wariness in his eyes.

"Oh, I reside in the city. I prefer the crowds of people and the excitement and tensions it creates. Why do you ask?"

"I thought it was the goal of most people to move out of the city streets and possess a bit of land like royalty."

He seemed to relax. "Yes, but if you read about them, the royals spend their time in the capital or attending gala affairs. The country is but a brief escape."

"Is that what you read?"

"No, not really. I tend to read the economic journals. Astrophysics For People In A Hurry is my current read. What about you?"

"During my work hours, there is little time. I'm usually reading work related journals or papers." She swallowed more of her coffee. Strange, Alex had barely touched his.

"You don't read anything else?"

"Rarely, there just isn't time. Today I caught up on household chores I've neglected and tomorrow will probably mean a couple hours of emailing people at work."

"Are you then indispensable?"

Raven laughed. "No, not really. Would you like to take in a movie or just take a walk around a small village? I could then show you my favorite night walk."

He stood. "The night walk sounds grand. Lead on, fair lady."

"It is a bit of a drive. It will be easier to take my pickup on the back roads, if you don't mind my driving."

"Not at all." Relief flooded his face.

He did hold the door for her as they walked outside and to the back lot where her pickup was parked.

"It won't matter if you leave yours here. As you can see the place isn't crowded at night, although some stop by after the movie is over."

She pressed the key to unlock her truck door and then opened the door. She tossed her purse behind the seat.

Alex opened the other door and boosted up on the passenger seat. "My, this is quite comfy. Leather seats. I didn't expect that."

"Haven't you ridden in a pickup truck before? They have all the comforts of a luxury auto."

He shrugged. "No, I don't believe I have. At least, not in, uh, recent years." Once again it was that odd choice of words. Raven checked for incoming or outgoing vehicles and pulled out of the parking lot.

"I'll swing by our park and community building before heading to the back roads." She turned right and went east for a couple of blocks. "The park starts on the right and the community building is on the left. Note those huge rocks as the base. The CCC built that back in the depths of the Great Depression. They didn't have anything like that during this depression, even though there was another Democrat in office. They rescued the bankers and financial institutions instead."

He looked at her and then at the rocks. She flipped a U-turn and headed back toward the main drag. Was it her imagination or did his face look more luminous in the dark?

"How did they get all those rocks there?"

"Some say they hauled them up from the river, but I don't know."

She turned onto the county road and then pulled over to a turn out. "There is one of my walks, but that isn't the one we'll do tonight. It is too short and it is still too early. Too many headlights."

She was pointing at a separate, narrow road and to an old fashioned metal bridge. Alex looked at it and then back at her.

She was smiling. "The county had to widen and move the road, but the bridge is a classic. It goes over the Snoqualmie River. During certain months, you can see people fishing down there."

"How did you discover this?"

She shrugged and put the truck back on the road. "When the realty person was showing me different places. I opted not to be on the river. I don't have time to be trapped by flooding." This time she chose a road that went upward.

"There's a great view from the top too, but it will soon be gone. I understand the land is for sale. Too bad I didn't win the lottery. I'd buy it."

"Land is that expensive here?" Alex asked.

"Of course, all those software companies pay such huge salaries that the housing market jacks prices higher every year."

At the top, she stopped the truck. "Look straight out and you'll see what I mean."

"I'd rather look at you, my dear." Alex had turned toward her, but he was too late. She was already stepping out of the cab. She closed the door and she felt the rays of the full moon dancing through her skin, rippling her muscles.

The soothing dark of night enclosed her. She leaned forward as she heard the sound of the other door opening and closing and the crunch of feet on the rocks and dirt as the man came around the front and she bared her teeth.

"Where did you go to? I thought we," and his voice stopped. The sight of her yellow eyes stunned him just long enough and she launched herself through the air, her wolf jaws and teeth clamping on his neck and tearing it away from the bone.

Raven knew she had to sever the neck and head. Her yellow eyes had caught the gleam of his long fangs. She was surprised at the amount of dark blood flowing from his body, but she did not stop to feast. This one was not for eating. Her weight wasn't enough to keep him on the ground and his arms pushed up his body and then he contorted and moved upward. Part of his neck was in her mouth, and she dropped to the ground snarling, gathering her hind quarter muscles to leap again. She saw him stagger and knew not whether it was from loss of blood or the flopping head. He still had those fangs and she growled.

He managed to lift his head and the elongated eye teeth gleamed in the moonlight as he flew at her. She turned and hurtled into the woods, slipping behind the fallen limbs of a hemlock tree. She slunk around the fallen trunk. He appeared staggering into the woods and she was up on the trunk and leaping at his side. He twisted to meet her charge and the force of her landing threw him to the ground and impaled a limb through his side and through his ribs to his heart. His body quivered and stilled.

She backed away. Her mind feared that creature that tried to end her night journeys. She sat on the ground, lifted her head, and howled. When she stood, she knew she needed to rid the earth of the sight of him, but the ground here was difficult to dig. She remembered trying to bury part of a coyote once. She trotted around the downed tree and its branches. The ground was softer by the middle of the tree and she began to dig. When finished, she trotted back to the body and grabbed him by the belt. It was awkward dragging him but she finally managed by the time the moon had sailed to the South.

It was another difficult task to throw enough dirt to cover him. A shoulder still protruded when she began to pull the dead branches over and around him. She feared sleeping here. If the stake held true she was safe. She slunk off down through a gully. She had to hide until dawn's light.

Raven walked back to her truck and retrieved the key from the floor. It puzzled her as to why he hadn't just jumped in the truck and drove off instead of attacking her. She walked around to where the body was hidden, and saw a bit of sunlight cutting through the branches. Where the sun hit was dust. A sigh of relief escaped and she headed back to the pickup. She had an email box full of work items that she needed to run through. Then she could tell Emma about the park, the walk on the bridge, and how one midnight walk with Alex was enough.

About the Author
Mari Collier

Mari Collier was born and raised on a farm in Iowa. From there she moved to Phoenix, then to North Bend, WA. When she retired, she found refuge in a small community in the high desert of California. She is an active member of the Twentynine Palms Historical Society and is on their Board of Directors. She writes two columns for the Old Schoolhouse Journal and enjoys family, friends, the local art galleries, and theaters.

Books by Mari Collier:

Earthbound
Gather The Children
Before We Leave
Return of the Maca
Thalia and Earth
Fall and Rise of the Macas
Twisted Tales from the Northwest
Twisted Tales from the Universe
Twisted Tales from the Desert
Twisted Tales from a Skewed Mind
Man, True Man

Links:

Facebook:
https://www.facebook.com/Mari-Collier-205325882886976/
Twitter: https://twitter.com/child7mari
Website: http://maricollier.com/

Shadow

Kat Wells

Esh paced across the wooden decking, lit by the moon"s brightness, still holding the letter in his hands that had summoned him there. Brief words, with no signature: the usual style, though it was true he hadn"t received one in some time.

The dockside was empty, the sailors already bedded down for the night, or otherwise occupied elsewhere. The only thing near was his shadow and the only sounds the lapping of inky waves against rotting, weed-encrusted deck boards and the far-off hum of tavern patrons singing in their drunken stupors.

Kivuli watched his master, listening to every step he took, knowing that soon someone would join them. Malkov. Kivuli"s dark form paled slightly at the thought, for Malkov was a man who commanded complete obedience, an obedience that his master, against his better judgement, found impossible not to give.

A second set of footsteps sounded in the night. Esh stopped his pacing. A figure was approaching, walking erect and with purpose. As the light hit him, Kivuli saw his face. Strong cheekbones jutted on either side, and his hair was long and straight, framing eyes so bright that they seemed to burn with an inner fire. A perfectly trimmed goatee sprung from his chin, and despite the warmth of the night he wore a thick cloak, and held a polished black walking cane at his side. He stopped in front of Esh, who bowed low before him, licking his dry lips. "You have a task for me, my Lord?" Esh asked, his tone hushed.

Malkov said nothing. Instead he looked around, and his bright eyes locked on Kivuli for the faintest of seconds, boring down on him as if he knew that the shadow was more than a grey form on the floor. He turned back to Esh. "You were not followed?"

"Of course not, my Lord," Esh replied. "My methods are not so lax, even if it has been some time since I last had need of them."

"Good. I was afraid you might have become…rusty…over the years. You know your skills have served me well in the past. I must call on them again."

Kivuli stretched away from Esh, unable to stand Malkov"s terrible presence. He suddenly felt someone beside him and jumped back, merging with the shadows of the docks.

"Calm yourself, Kivuli, it is only I," a voice said next to him.

Kivuli recognised it. It was the same as Malkov"s, but there was no hint of hardness in it. "Ombra?" he asked.

"Indeed. Surely you were expecting me? After all, is it not my master with whom yours now speaks?"

"I – It didn"t occur to me," Kivuli said. "You know how your master makes me feel. I can"t concentrate on anything when he"s near."

Ombra gave a low chuckle. "You should take comfort then, Kivuli, for there are many who fear him. There are times when even I tremble in his presence."

"Truly? You"re afraid of your own master?"

"He is cruel and ruthless. If he does not get what he wants, his anger is unquenchable. It would be folly not to fear him."

"But what does he want? My master"s carried out tasks for him twice now, and both times he came across danger. If this new request is anything like those, then I can"t bare to think of what might happen to him. I"ve got to help him, Ombra, For his own sake," Kivuli said.

"No." It was one word, but it struck Kivuli silent. "You know our laws, Kivuli. You must never reveal yourself to him. Never let the humans know what we are capable of. Only a fool would think of exposing us."

Without a word more, Ombra slid away to his master, who now turned away from Esh and strode back into the darkness of the night. Esh stayed for a while, watching the tide swell in and out, but eventually grew tired. With Kivuli behind him, they made their way to the squalid streets of town.

Half-clad women called out to Esh as he travelled the back alleys, keen to stay away from more reputable eyes, flashing what little skin was still covered by their threadbare clothes. Kivuli knew Esh had no taste for their unwashed lips tonight, not now he had a job to do. Besides, even the times when he did partake in their company, Kivuli couldn"t help but feel it was only his master"s way of suppressing the thoughts that forever haunted him.

They took their usual, winding path to Esh"s home, which, so far, not even the most skilled pickpockets and spies had managed to follow. They came out by a rotten staircase that jutted out into a minor street. Esh darted up it and unlocked the door at the top.

It was black inside, but he struck a match and lit an oil lamp just inside the door. It revealed the narrow corridor they were in, leading to a single door. Inside, the room was small, with a straw mattress at one end, and a crude wooden desk and chair at the other. A fireplace was set into the back wall, while a basin stood in the corner, with a jug of clean water and a cloth resting on the side. Papers littered the floor. Most of them were sketches of people Esh had been commissioned to track at one time or another, others were old journals and childish scribblings once belonging to his wife and daughter, lost so many years ago from plague as they"d crossed the sea to the mainland, with the hope of living a more prosperous life.

Kivuli missed their shadows, how they had laughed and played and grown together. His family. It was seven years that moon since they"d been lost, their life extinguished along with their masters". He and Esh had been immune. Watching them die was one thing neither of them would ever forget, no matter how much they wished to.

Esh picked up one of his daughter"s scribblings, tracing the ink marks with his fingertips, before letting it drop from his grasp to drift back to the floor. He slumped down in the chair, his head dropping to rest on the rough grain of the desk. Kivuli looked on from where he stood against the wall, blending in with the darkness of the room, wishing that he was more than a shadow, wishing he could break the laws binding him so he could help his master. Whatever Malkov had planned for Esh, it wasn"t good. Kivuli knew it, down in his very being. He had to do something.

The sun had risen high before Kivuli saw his master begin to stir. Realising how late it was, Esh jumped up, knocking over the desk he"d fallen asleep at. He splashed some water on his face, running a hand through his hair, and put on a clean cotton tunic, woollen jacket and trousers.

Throwing one last glance at the scattered papers, which Kivuli lingered by in the light, he strode from the room, down the corridor and out into the morning air, already stagnant with the reek of soiled foods, sweat and seaweed.

They headed to a run-down tavern in the centre of town, far from Esh"s usual place to meet clients. The smell of spilled ale and stale vomit emanating up from the straw-covered floor made Esh"s brow sweat. Kivuli looked around at the other customers, and noticed that both men and shadow alike had an unsavoury aura. Shaking a little, he stayed close to his master, who had chosen to sit in the corner, as far away from them as he could get.

A serving girl, little more than a child, came over to see what Esh wanted. She wore a dress so patched and filthy that it was hard to tell what the original colour might have been. Kivuli caught several eyes ogling her from across the room. He shuddered, noticing Esh do the same. The girl was only a few years old than his daughter had been when she died. To be working in a place like this...

"Ale," Esh answered to her unasked question. She nodded and went to fetch it.

As she came back, spilling most of it on the floor as rowdy patrons jostled and knocked against her, Kivuli saw a man walk in wearing a rough-spun cloak. The hood concealed most of his face, but on seeing Esh he lowered it to reveal an angular jaw and a nose that had the tell-tale slant of having been broken at some point. He walked over, grinning as though meeting an old friend, but Kivuli was sure his master had never met him before. He looked around for the man"s shadow, and saw it just a little way away from him. It too was angular, and Kivuli didn"t recognise it.

"Fancy seein" you ere, friend," the man said, sitting down at the table next to Esh. His voice was slurred, with a dryness to it that Kivuli didn"t like. Then he put his hands on the table and interlaced his fingers, dropping both index fingers down quickly and then up again.

Esh swallowed and held his arm half under the table, rolling up his sleeve to reveal three silvery scars, slashed through with a fourth. Malkov"s mark, received six years ago as a reward for surviving the first task he"d been set. The man grunted, and drew a small bundle from inside his cloak, passing it to Esh under the table. Kivuli moved closer to look at it, but the man"s shadow clawed out at him with a hiss. He drew back quickly, just as the man got up again.

"Sorry ta leave ya already, friend," he said. "Tho I "spect we"ll be seein" each other soon enuff." He turned away, hiding his face under his hood once more, and left the tavern. Esh and Kivuli watched him leave, but no one else spared him a second glance.

Five minutes later, Esh downed his ale and left a coin on the table for the serving girl to collect, before leaving himself.

Back in their room, Esh opened the bundle. Inside was a bag containing a strange powder, and a scrap of paper. Putting the powder aside, he unfolded the paper and read, mumbling the words loud enough for Kivuli to hear. "Ignite the powder when all is done. Do not ready it until the switch has been made. Do not dally, we shall be watching." He inhaled deeply and scrunched the paper in his hand, throwing it against the wall. It bounced off and landed on top of one of his wife"s journals.

Seeing it, his eyes suddenly turned watery, and he sank to his knees, putting his head in his hands. "Please, Maggie," he sobbed, tears dripping through his fingers. "Please... don"t judge me too much... "

His sobbing went on until Kivuli was sure there were no more tears left for his master to shed. Then, with a look of crazed anger, Esh smashed his fist against the floor. Gathering the journals up, he threw them onto the hearth and took a match from his pocket, ready to strike it.

"Stop!"

Esh froze, the match hovering inches from the friction paper. "Who... who said that? Is someone there?" He wiped his face roughly on his sleeve, pocketing the match again, and went over to the door, thrusting it open to stare down the corridor. When he saw no-one there, he went back to the fireplace. Kivuli tried to keep silent, but then his master struck the match.

"No, master, please!"

Kivuli couldn"t stop himself. His master was a good man, he didn"t deserve to be dragged down by the likes of Malkov and his men.

"Who"s there?" Esh said again, his skin paling.

Kivuli shook slightly, but he had made his choice. Speaking to one"s master was forbidden, no matter what the circumstance, but Esh was too important for him to care. "Master, please. Look at the wall next to you," Kivuli said. In the light coming from the window, his outline was distinct against the wall. His master looked at him, still uncomprehending. "Master, I am your shadow."

Silence. Esh didn"t move or waver so much as an inch, despite the match burning down to his fingertips. He just stood, staring at Kivuli, his expression unchanged. At last he spoke, wetting his lips with his tongue. "My shadow?" He walked closer to the wall and held out his hand, touching Kivuli lightly as though he might suddenly attack.

"Yes, master," Kivuli whispered. He lifted his arm independently, with deliberate slowness so as not to cause more alarm. His master's eyes followed it, growing wide and glistening slightly.

"No. This isn't real. Just a trick of the light, that's all. Or there was something in that ale... you can't move on your own, and you certainly can't talk on your own either."

"Please Master, I understand that this is a shock, but you must listen."

Esh tightened his lips together and shook his head. Kivuli sighed. He walked around the room, moving from wall to wall and across the floor, merging with the static shadows and then reappearing again. "You see?" he said.

Esh had seen. He grabbed for the wooden chair and slumped down on it heavily, still watching Kivuli with a wild look in his eyes. "How...?" he breathed.

"That doesn't matter. Please, you must reconsider your involvement with Malkov."

"Malkov?" Esh said, blinking. "I'd forgotten."

"Master, I've spoken with Malkov's shadow—"

"His shadow can speak too?"

"All shadows belonging to living creatures can speak," Kivuli said softly. "Those that can speak the human tongue, at least. Malkov's shadow is called Ombra, and even he fears him. I have no doubt that Malkov thinks of you as expendable."

Esh stood up and picked up a dusty wineskin from under the straw mattress. He opened it and took a long drink, wiping his mouth after. He took a few steps away from Kivuli, but then turned back to him. "I know that Malkov's using me. And I know he's dangerous. But tell me, shadow of mine, what is it I'm supposed to do? If I survive this job, I'll earn enough money to go back home and escape this place... and leave my pain behind. And if I back out now, he'll only hunt me down."

"Then go to him first."

Esh laughed. A desperate, pitying sound. "That would be suicide."

"Not necessarily. Malkov is a man who expects to get what he wants. If you hold your ground, you'll surprise him. He might just let you go."

"He might... or he might not." Esh paced around some more. "Damn it! Alright, shadow, have it your way. I'm probably dead anyway."

Kivuli and Esh watched Malkov"s house from where they sat in wait in the tavern opposite, in the rich quarter of town. It was the evening Esh was due to carry out Malkov"s plans, and they knew that soon the rest of Malkov"s men would be leaving to set everything up...and Malkov himself would be alone.

Two hours passed before the grand doors of the house opened, and five men came out, making their way down the street. With a slight tremor, Kivuli noticed the man Esh had met at the other tavern, hovering at the back of the group, with his shadow snapping at its fellows.

Waiting until they turned the corner and disappeared from sight, Kivuli and Esh left the relative safety of the tavern and went outside to Malkov"s house. Following Kivuli"s plan to surprise him, they avoided the main door and went around to the side, where they knew the entrance to the cellars was. Esh had been marked down there. It wasn"t a memory easily erased.

When they reached it, they found the gate locked and chained - no more than they"d expected. Esh took out a thin knife and a stolen hairpin to try and pick it open. To help him, Kivuli slid his hand into the lock and told him which way it needed to be turned. A moment later, it clicked open, and they descended into the cellar.

The void inside hit them sharply, and for a moment Kivuli was lost in it. Searching around the wooden crates and barrels stored around them, he felt about until his dark hands brushed lumps of melted wax. Tracing it upwards, his fingers closed around the stump of a candle, with just enough wick left on it to light. He rolled it over to Esh, where it bumped against his boots. Esh lit it immediately, and filled the room with a warm, flickering glow. With the staircase to the main house now illuminated, they went up, coming out into the hall. There they paused, hiding behind a large, marble bust on a pedestal, listening for any signs of Malkov.

Loud voices were coming from a room further down, and a manservant came running from it, holding a blood-soaked cloth to his arm. Kivuli and Esh shrank back as he passed, but then edged down the hall to peer through the door.

"I should have had a report back by now," they heard Malkov say. "Something is wrong. Even from here, we should have heard an explosion." He sounded panicked, and the dominance had completely disappeared from his voice.

"You fret much, Malkov. All shall go to plan."

"But you said his shadow was concerned. What if he suspected we were setting Esh up to be framed for it. If he talked him out—"

"Kivuli does not possess the courage to break the Laws of Shadow. A simple word from myself kept those thoughts of his at bay. He would never reveal himself to Esh." It was Ombra speaking.

Before he knew what he was doing, Kivuli had slipped into the room. There they were; Malkov, sitting in a fur-backed chair near the fire, his eyes now dull and his goatee untrimmed. Ombra was on the wall next to him, stretched out to his largest form, distorted so much that he barely resembled Malkov at all.

"Ombra? Kivuli said.

Malkov sat up, startled by the voice. He looked around, and his eyes locked on Esh, as he, too, stepped inside the room. "You!" he said, half-standing, but Ombra silenced him.

"It seems I have made a grave error, Kivuli. You are obviously not the coward I took you for...to think you broke our laws so easily. I have to say, I am somewhat impressed. You, however," he said, rounding on Malkov, who seemed to melt into his chair; every sign of the confident tyrant they"d taken him to be gone from his composure. "You assured me that this scoundrel of a man would be too fearful to back out."

"Ombra, this was all you?" Kivuli asked, the disbelief only too clear in his voice. "Why?"

"How many thousands of years have we shadows been but mere attachments, shackled to these buffoons but never able act upon our own will? Silenced for fear of alarming them?" Ombra hissed. "Well, I say no more. It is time for change, Kivuli. Humans are weak and filled with greed and hatred, we can let ourselves be ruled by them no longer. We must strive to be the masters now." He slid over to Malkov, who withdrew even more. "It is a sad thing that my life is forever tied to yours," he whispered. "If it were not so, I would have killed you long ago. As it is, I must instead command you to dispose if these two fools. Hesitate, and I shall do so myself. You will find the sight far less pleasant."

Malkov got up shakily and drew a rapier down from its display on the wall above the fireplace. Despite being used for an ornament, Kivuli could see the point was still sharp. He glanced at Malkovs"s face. The man"s eyes had grown glassy; his heart was not in it. Still, Kivuli couldn"t see a way to stop him, and with Ombra controlling him, words were useless. He looked at his master, who stood still despite Malkov"s advancement. He caught a slight bulge in Esh"s jacket pocket.

Suddenly, he knew.

He swept up and whispered something in Esh"s ear, speaking quickly.

"But what"ll happen to you?" Esh whispered back.

"Don"t worry, master. Please, you have no time!"

"Then at least tell me your name, shadow. I haven"t even asked," Esh said urgently.

"It"s Kivuli."

Nodding slightly, Esh dipped his hand into his jacket pocket, withdrawing the powder that had been in the bundle. As Malkov readied his rapier to strike, Esh charged at him, ducking under his sword arm and driving him back into Ombra with as much force as he could muster. Then he threw the powder into the fire beside them. The flames leapt up, birthing forth a brilliant, blinding light, engulfing them all.

It hit Ombra full on. The shadow let out a roar of undiluted agony...and vanished.

The powder"s effects finally dulled, but it was an hour before both Malkov and Esh had recovered their sight. When they were at last able to look around, they found both Kivuli and Ombra missing.

"Have they both...gone?" Malkov asked, searching the whole room. Only static shadows surround them.

"I think so," Esh said. He sighed.

"Why so solemn, master?" Kivuli"s voice came, sounding faintly amused. "Could it be that you felt a loss for me?"

"Kivuli? Where...where are you?" Esh asked.

"Open your jacket, master."

Esh did so, and Kivuli"s grey form poured out of it and onto the floor.

"And Ombra?" Malkov breathed.

"He is truly gone," Kivuli said. "There was no chance for him to hide as I did. You are a free man, now. Though," he added, snaking over to him, "I have one request for you. Release my master from your service and fund his journey home. We"ve both had more than our share of horrors in this place."

About the Author
Kat Wells

Kathryn Wells is a writer of fantasy, children's fiction, short stories and poetry. As a child, she found her passion for the written word, and even though she had many other interests growing up, writing was always the one she would return to. Her stories are often laugh out loud funny, with plenty of magic and as many whimsical touches as possible, but if you look closely, darkness often lurks between the lines...

Books by Kat Wells:

Unofficial Detective

Links:

Website: http://www.kathrynwells.co.uk/

A Shade of Hope

Natalie J Case

Leaning against the stone of the ancient wall that became a bridge over what had once been a busy river, Raven Ivany tried to make it look like she was just any other tourist, maybe waiting for a companion to return from the nearby café with coffee. She scanned the area before glancing back down at her phone. It was nearly midnight.

She pushed off the wall and started down the gentle incline toward the walkway along the river, letting the shadow cast by the bridge swallow her. She didn't mind the dark. Her eyes picked out details others would miss, even in the pitch black. She was a Shade after all, and darkness was her home. She sighed when she didn't see anyone lurking there waiting for her.

The text message had been ominous, if a little vague on the details. She almost didn't come, but her curiosity had gotten the better of her. "Midnight, under the bridge. Come alone," was the entire text, from an unknown number, and considering her own phone was a prepaid disposable she'd only picked up three days before, she was intrigued.

Raven paced a little, watching the numbers on her phone climb closer to midnight. She was mildly on edge after a very close call in Paris a few days prior. She'd been laying low in Poissy before attempting to go back to Paris to finish what she had started.

The sound of a hard leather soled shoe scuffing on gravel pulled her attention. A dark figure emerged from the shadows and moved toward her. He was lilting slightly to his left, one hand hidden under his jacket. He came to a stop about halfway through the dark space under the bridge and lifted the hand not currently holding his insides inside his body.

Raven could smell the blood. She moved closer cautiously, looking over the man. He was clearly on approach to middle-age, though he seemed fit enough. His dark hair was slicked back and his bland suit was wrinkled as though he'd been in it for more than a few days. "You sent the text?" she asked, holding her phone up.

He nodded. "Adam Darvin."

She raised an eyebrow and inched closer. "American?" He nodded. "And a fed." She didn't phrase it as a question, but he nodded to confirm her suspicions. "How bad?" She nodded toward his injury.

"Bad enough. We shouldn't stay here." He glanced behind him. Raven moved to look as well. "If we stay here, they will find us."

"Who is they?" Raven asked. "And what is this about?"

"I came to warn you." Darvin said, walking toward her. "There's a man hunting you."

"And you know this how?" Raven asked, turning to walk beside him. She couldn't decide if he was a threat or not, but figured the injury was bad enough that it put the favor on her side.

"I saw you in Paris. I know what you are."

She stiffened a little, but fought the urge to run. "I don't know what you mean."

He leaned in and licked his lips. "You're a Shade." His words were barely a whisper, but it made her quicken her pace. "I'm not here to hurt you, but I wasn't the only one who saw what you did."

"Is that who hurt you?" Raven asked.

Darvin stumbled and reached out to her, his bloody hand grabbing her arm. "Yes, and he isn't far behind me." He pulled on her arm. "Look, leave me here if you don't trust me, or help me stop leaving a blood trail he can follow and we can find a place to lay low. I'll tell you everything."

She knew it was stupid, and she knew her grandfather wouldn't be happy, but she also couldn't leave the man like he was. She drew him to a bench. "Sit. Give me a minute." He sat, moving his suit jacket so she could get a better look. She sank down to a squat beside the bench. Exhaling slowly and glancing around to make sure they wouldn't be observed, Raven lifted her hand and hovered it over the wound. It was deep and nearly six inches wide. It was going to need a whole lot more work than she was capable of here in the open.

"Okay, I can close the wound, but it needs a more work than I can do here. You've got internal bleeds and.... it's not good."

"I guessed that."

She glanced up at him. He was starting to succumb to the shock. "Alright. Stay with me. I'll get this sealed and we can get out of here." She turned her attention to the wound, tracing a hand along its path. She closed her eyes and felt her way inside, pulling the skin together and urging healing energy into it. When she opened her eyes, there was only a red line where the wound had been. Darvin's eyes were closed and she reached a hand to his shoulder to rouse him. "You were the one who said we needed to move. Let's go."

He lurched up and she moved to his good side, slipping an arm around his waist, her hand hovering near the wound to monitor it. He settled his right arm around her shoulders and they set off down the riverside path, looking like two lovers on their way home.

Raven glanced behind them as they neared the turn that would take them back toward the small set of rooms where her grandfather and sister were sleeping. She couldn't see anyone who might be following. "Okay, it isn't far now." It was risky, taking him there, but she really couldn't see another option. He was fading fast.

She got him down the alley to their door and managed to get him inside without waking the entire street, but then she struggled. He was heavy and losing consciousness. Suddenly there was a second pair of hands and her grandfather's voice. "And who might this be?"

"Long story, he's been stabbed. I didn't think I should risk healing him out in the open, not after Paris."

He grunted in agreement and helped her guide the fed to the couch. They got him laying down so that his wounded side was accessible and her grandfather knelt on the floor, opening the man's shirt before laying his hand over the wound. His eyes closed and she could feel his energy sinking into Darvin's skin.

His head lifted, but his eyes stayed closed. "Bring me some water."

Raven nodded and slipped into the small kitchen and reached for a glass, filling it and taking to him. She put it in his outreached hand and he drank it down, handing her the glass back. "And some for him now."

She refilled the glass and came back, surprised to see Darvin's eyes open. She slipped to her knees near his head, dipping her finger into the water to stir it with healing energy before she leaned in, holding the glass with one hand and lifting Darvin's head with the other. "Drink all of it." Raven murmured, helping him until the glass was nearly empty. She glanced aside at what her grandfather was doing, nodding as she followed his energy deep into the man's body.

"He is taking care of the bleeds, but it will take more than one treatment to get you back on your feet. You should sleep."

Darvin's eyes moved from her to her grandfather and back. He nodded slightly. His eyes closed and she turned her attention back to the work her grandfather was doing. After a few minutes she felt him pull his energy back and he pushed himself up to his feet. He pulled her back to the kitchen with a hand on hers. "Who is he?"

Raven shrugged, moving away to fill the kettle with water for tea. "Said his name was Adam Darvin." He wasn't going to like that she went out to meet him, or that he worked for the United States Federal Government. "Where are Manny and Rose?"

"Don't change the subject." He came to her and took her hand, patting it gently. "Raven, we must be careful. The world is not like Shady Lake. There are those who would hurt us if they knew what we were."

She sighed and cupped a hand to his cheek. "I know, Papa, but I couldn't leave him on the streets to die." She turned to pull tea cups from the cupboard and set them on the counter. "Besides, I think he wants to help. He was the one who texted me. He wanted to warn us."

"Warn us?" He stepped back to look through the open doorway at Darvin.

"He didn't go into details, but he said someone saw us in Paris and that's who shoved a knife in his stomach."

"And you bring him here?" He shook his head and paced away toward the door. "Okay, he can stay until the morning, he should be healed enough to go then. With any luck, Rose and Manny find what we're looking for and we'll move on."

Raven felt her chest tighten. "Did you find him?"

He sighed heavily. "We'll know when they get back. Manny was pretty sure when they left."

They'd been looking for a long time. The search had taken them to London, then Manchester before coming south through Calais on the ferry, chasing a lead that her mother had spent time in Paris. Then they had learned that a man her mother had risked her life to heal was in Poissy, which was what had brought them here.

Her mother had been missing since she was twelve and Rose was fourteen. She had left ostensibly to see to her dying mother who had been living in London. She called after the funeral, saying she was going to visit some family before coming home.

They hadn't heard from her again. Their father had gone looking more than once, the last time he'd been killed in a car accident in Manchester. When Raven had turned eighteen, they had come to find her or find out what had happened to her.

Raven poured tea and handed a cup to her grandfather before sinking to a seat at the table. They sipped at it quietly before the door opened and Rose came in with Manny behind her. Manny put his hands on her grandfather's shoulders and kissed the top of his head. "Well, we found our dear cousin Frederick." Rose said, snagging Raven's tea cup and drinking from it. "But he had no idea where Mom went after Paris."

Her red hair was tightly braided except for the one strand that her fingers played with alongside her face.

"Did he at least tell you what it was she was doing?"

Manny moved to pour tea for him and Rose, shaking his head. "He said your grandmother asked her to find her sister and when Anna took her last breath, it included a pretty strong compulsion to finish the task."

"Aunt Vivian?" Raven asked, her eyes squinting as she tried to remember the woman. Her only memory was from a time when she was six or seven and her mother's sister had visited them for Christmas. She was tall and mysterious and Raven remembered that she'd smelled of eucalyptus and mint. Unlike the family on Raven's father's side, Aunt Vivian was stand-offish and didn't seem to want anything to do with either Raven or Rose.

"Apparently there was something very important Grandmother wanted Aunt Vivian to know."

Raven sipped at her tea, digging through her memory for anything ever said about her aunt. "Didn't Dad once say that Aunt Vivian was mixed up in some crazy conspiracy? Something about a hidden Shade history?"

Rose rolled her eyes. "Yeah, Frederick had something to say about that too. Mostly that Aunt Vivian was a few fries short of a happy meal."

"That's no way to talk about your aunt," their grandfather chided. "But this was our last clue. I think it's time we head home. Raven has a Book of Line she should be copying, and Rose has school starting again soon."

"What about..." Raven gestured toward the living room where their guest was sleeping. "If someone is looking for us, do we want to lead them home?"

"What?" Rose asked, leaning back so she could see into the room. "Who is he?"

Raven shrugged. "Adam Darvin, government agent of some kind. He knew what I was, said someone saw me with that kid in Paris."

"I told you." Rose said, her hand dropping onto Raven's. "You're too soft, little sister. It's going to get you into trouble."

"In the morning I will book us on a night flight out of Paris." Manny said. "We can fly into New York, rent a van. Somebody wants to try to follow the way I drive, let them." He smirked and winked at Raven. "I'll drop Rose at school and you two back home, then I'll drive the van out to Los Angeles. I can use some of my frequent flier miles to come back."

His hand slipped over to cover her grandfather's. It was an odd relationship, a non-Shade and a Shade as gifted as her grandfather, but Manny had been a part of their lives as long as she could remember, and the love between them was palpable.

Part of her wanted to stay, to keep looking, but part of her knew that if her mother didn't want to be found, she wouldn't be. She finished her tea and stood. "I'll check in on our guest, see if I can add to what Grandpa did earlier. The sooner we get him on his way, the sooner we can go."

* * *

The late afternoon sun leaked around the curtains in the living room, and Raven skirted around it to move back to the couch with the glass of water. Darvin stirred, as if sensing her approach, his eyes opening. He looked at her, then the window. "What time is it?"

She shook her head and knelt beside the couch. "Almost three. You took a bad turn early this morning. Drink this."

He shifted so he could take the glass, draining it and handing it back. "How?"

"Whatever he used to stab you, it tore you up inside. You were lucky I was sitting here when the bleeds broke again. My grandfather does good work, but they were deep and barely closed when he was done."

71

She shifted to sit on the floor, setting the glass on the small table beside him. "At one point, I think you actually died, I was chasing after an elusive bleeder and I felt you go. But my grandfather came out and we brought you back."

Raven stifled a yawn and blinked tired eyes.

"You should be asleep." Darvin said, moving to sit up properly.

"I wasn't going to leave you here to die on our couch." Raven countered stretching. "However, you seem to be doing much better. "She held a hand up and looked him in the eye. "May I?"

He nodded and she covered the developing scar, closing her eyes as she checked through all of the work they'd done and infused the area with more energy. "Good. I'd say you're ready to go."

"Just like that?" Darvin asked.

"Did you have something else in mind?" Raven asked with a frown.

His eyes met hers. "Tell me about your mother."

She stiffened and stood. "You shouldn't have heard any of that."

"I have good ears." Darvin stood slowly, one hand holding his side. He seemed to test the work they'd done, shifting his weight and nodding his head. "How long has she been missing?"

"Six years next month." Raven said.

"Give me a place to start, and I'll find her for you." Darvin said. "It is what I do. I find Shades, and other…types of unusual folks. If she can be found, I will find her."

"I don't think…" She looked to the hallway. Her grandfather didn't really have to know. He wouldn't approve of an outsider digging into what he deemed to be family business. Raven crossed back to the side table and picked up a dog-eared notebook with tabs on the top and side. "This is everything I know about where she's been and what she's done."

He took it and paged through it, nodding. "Good. How do I find you?"

She smiled. "You found me here. I'm sure you can find me back home."

He chuckled, nodding. "I suppose I should be getting out of here, let you get some sleep."

Raven lifted a clean shirt from the nearby chair. "A gift from Manny. You two are close to the same size. It should hold you over until you get wherever you're going."

Darvin's eyebrow raised and he took the shirt, dropping his bloodstained and torn shirt to the couch and slipping into the new one. He took his jacket from the arm of the couch and fished something out of his inner pocket. He held out a card to here. "If you think you might want a job, after you finish with your Book of Line, call me."

Raven took the card and looked it over before looking at him with suspicion. The card had no federal agency name, no indication that it was associated with the government at all. It was just his name and a phone number. "What kind of job are you offering?"

He grinned. "I'm afraid that's classified. But I can promise you it will play to your talents. And, we'll train you. I can already tell you have some of the skills."

She raised an eyebrow. "What makes you think I'd be interested?"

"Call it a hunch." He pulled the jacket on and headed toward the kitchen, and the door out. She stood in the living room turning the card over in her hand.

Raven sighed and tiptoed around the sunlight leaking through the curtains, slipping through the half open door of the room she shared with her sister. She tucked the card into her worn canvas backpack and slipped into bed, sleep already pulling at her.

In the small space of twenty-four hours, everything had changed, and nothing had changed at the same time. She would go home and do her duty. But when that was over? She had no desire to try to disguise her powers under the guise of some medical worker, no desire of the long nights of schooling it would take.

Now she had another choice. She closed her eyes. It wasn't anything she had ever considered before, but now that Darvin had pointed out the path, Raven knew she'd be calling him one day.

About the Author
Natalie J Case

An avid reader from a very early age, Natalie grew up in worlds that only exist in books. Her influences run the gamut of genres, from childhood mysteries like Nancy Drew and The Bobsey Twins to epic fantasy and hardcore sci-fi.

A Shade of Hope is a slice of backstory from her paranormal thriller series, *Shades and Shadows*. The first two books in that series, *Through Shade and Shadow* and *In Gathering Shade,* were released in 2017. She is currently working on finishing up that series with *Where Shadows Fall,* due out in 2018.

Books by Natalie J Case:

Forever
Through Shade and Shadow
In Gathering Shade

Links:

Facebook: https://www.facebook.com/authornataliejcase/
Twitter: http://twitter.com/nataliejcase
Website: https://nataliejcase.com/

Ra-Kit's Initiation

W. Bradford Swift

Not long after their first eco-adventure, where Zak spoke with passion and commitment to the world leaders at the World Environmental Summit urging them to mend their ways before it was too late, he found himself with his new friend and eco-teammate, Sampson the flying dog, lounging around the park across from his home, recuperating from a very trying few weeks.

Eventually, he got up the nerve to ask the question that he'd had since first meeting Ra-Kit who claimed to be the last magic cat on earth. They'd met at the animal hospital where Zak's canine companion, Angus, had been brought after being hit by a car. Ra-Kit saved Angus' life only to turn around and blackmail Zak into helping her with the mission to speak for humans at the World Environmental.

Zak took a moment to clear his throat before asking the question. "Sampson, do you mind if I ask you a question that has been burning a hole in my mind for weeks?"

"Sure, Zak, fire away," Sampson replied, rolling over on the grass so he could better see his new friend.

"Well, you've been with Ra-Kit for quite a few years, right?"

"Yes, that's right," Sampson replied.

"Have you been her companion since the very beginning?"

"Oh, no," Sampson replied. "We've been together for several decades but not from the beginning. Why do you ask?"

Zak paused, trying to think of the best way to ask the question, then decided the direct approach would be best.

"I was just wondering, how Ra-Kit became a magic cat? I mean, was she born with her magical powers, or what?"

Sampson chuckled at the question. "Well, I don't know that anyone knows for absolute certainty how that came about, but I can tell you the generally accepted story—the one that's on file at the Animal's Spiritual Frontier. I guess you could say it's the official version and the one I was directed to when I asked that same question not long after becoming Ra-Kit's companion. Would that be helpful?"

"Yeah, that would be great," Zak replied, sitting up and plucking a blade of grass from the ground to chew on.

"Well, the story as I learned it starts back in the 1800s—1863 to be exact, when the cat that we now know as Ra-Kit was less than a year old..."

"Wait a minute. I thought she told me she was over five hundred years old," Zak said with a confused look on his face.

"Yeah, well, I've heard her refer to several different ages. She tends to be a little creative when it comes to her true age. All I know is the story I learned while visiting the Spiritual Frontier, which, like I said is the official version. Now, do you want to hear it or not?"

"Sure. Sorry. Go ahead," Zak said as he made a motion pretending to lock his lips shut.

"Good. As I was saying, the story begins in London, England in 1863 where a very young and precocious cat is trying to survive in a most troubling time.

* * *

The scrawled note had been ominous, if a little vague in the details. "Midnight, on the bridge. Come alone." Times were tough for everyone—two-legged and four-legged alike, but it was far worse to be on your own these days. So, Allie had followed the instructions. Now, look where she'd ended up.

"Quick with that cheese," Master Cat Beemer shouted to his crew. "No telling how long we have before the two-legs awaken and we have to scrub the whole mission." The other four cats that made up his gang nodded silently and bent that much harder to the task. Everyone knew the last thing you wanted was to get on Beemer's bad side. The only thing worse would be to get on Doggin's black list. If that happened, you'd be cut loose from the clan, then left to beg on the streets like the hundreds of other feral cats of London in 1863.

It was far better to lick a bulldog's boots, as it were, and to do what Doggin and his right-hand cat, Beemer, ordered. So, they all worked diligently to clean out the two-legs' pantry as fast as possible, which is probably why no one noticed the three mice watching their every move.

"Jaco, where's Allie? Didn't I tell you to keep an eye on her and make sure she survives her first outing?"

"Sorry, boss," Jaco replied without pausing from pushing a large loaf of bread towards the edge of the shelf. "She was here a minute ago. Said she needed to go check on something upstairs. I thought she'd be back by now."

"You idiot! You call that looking out after her? The only thing she's likely to find upstairs are two-legs, and that'll be nothing but trouble for all of us. Stay here and make sure no one slouches off. I've got to go find her. Doggin will have us all hanging from the watchtower if anything happens to her. He has great plans for our newest recruit."

* * *

Allie's sleek black coat made her a near perfect cat burglar. Her only short-comings were her misty green eyes that were so bright they almost glowed in the dark, but she'd learned early on to squint whenever necessary to keep the risk of detection to a minimum. She squinted now as she leapt to the top of the chest-of-drawer and just as she had hoped, found the ornately decorated box within which she felt sure she'd find the treasure that would place her in good stead with Doggin for years to come.

Her plan was simple. Find a two-leg's bauble that Doggin could trade in for the much more valuable commodity of food, thus demonstrating to him a much easier and more lucrative way to collect food. And her plan would have worked perfectly if it hadn't been for the blasted mice who were even now pattering across the two-legs' bed alerting them to the double burglary that was in process.

Allie sniffed around the top of the chest for a few moments. As best she could tell, the box wasn't even locked. She confirmed her conclusion by nudging the top open with her nose, revealing small compartments filled with baubles of every size and description. She reached for the shiniest one she could see—a simple ring with a single crystal-clear stone in its setting. Just as she grabbed it with her teeth, she felt a firm grasp on the nape of her neck as she was yanked away from the chest and thrown into a musty canvas bag. She struggled to regain her balance but couldn't get any solid footing. Tossed from side-to-side as she was carted away, she inhaled the dust from within the bag. She fought to keep from sneezing but knew it was just a matter of seconds before her natural instincts would take over. She took one final gulp and swallowed, then exhaled a final time in an attempt to blow the dust from her nose, but it was too little, too late. She sneezed and sneezed until she felt like she was about to turn inside out, but as soon as she finished one sneeze, the dust would return to her nose, and she'd have to sneeze again. Finally, her body appeared to adapt to the musty conditions and she laid quietly in the bag. The motion of the bag continued for several minutes. She didn't know where they were carrying her, but she doubted she'd be pleased with her new destination.

* * *

"Quick, everyone. Take what we have and let's scram!" Beemer shouted as he flew into the pantry. "The two-legs have Allie, and our goose is cooked if we don't get her back." The rest of his crew was experienced and trained to make quick getaways, which was why Doggin had assigned his youngest recruit to Beemer's gang. Now, he'd pay for it with his hide...unless he could somehow rescue her.

"Jaco, come with me," Beemer ordered. "The rest of you get this stuff back to Doggin. If he asks where we are, tell him we've been unavoidably detained, but assure him that we'll be back very soon, and under no circumstance, tell him what really happened. Show him how much we pilfered this evening. That should distract him long enough. We'll be back as soon as we can...hopefully with Allie."

The other three cats threw the half-full bag of food into the cart and pulled it away to their hideout, while Beemer and Jaco went looking for where the two-legs had taken Allie.

"Let's head to the river," Beemer said as he started off in that direction. "These two-legs don't have much imagination when it comes to exterminating cats. That's almost certainly the direction they've headed."

Sure enough, the two cats caught up with a tall two-legs carrying a burlap bag over his shoulder, a couple of inches of his nightgown sticking out below his overcoat. Even though it was only early September, the night temperatures were cold with the first hints of winter that was just around the corner. It was clear to Beemer that the two-leg meant to finish his business as quickly as possible, so he could get back to the warmth of his bed. So, he wasn't particularly surprised when the man reached the bridge and without a moment of hesitation tossed the bag with a squirming Allie into the cold, dirty water of the Thames. Without bothering to look down, the two-leg turned and retraced his steps.

"Quick, down this way to the river's edge. We have to keep an eye on that bag and pray that it stays afloat long enough for us to pull Allie to safety." Beemer ran around the edge of the bridge with Jaco close behind. What they saw didn't put their minds at ease. Already the burlap was collecting water and dipped under the waves before coming back up, then dipping under the surface again.

"Allie, keep fighting!" Beemer yelled. "We're here. We're going to get you out. You've got to stay afloat just a little longer."

"Down there," Jaco shouted, pointing to where a weeping willow hung over the river. "Maybe we can reach her from there."

"Let's go," Beemer replied as he streaked towards the tree in an effort to reach it before the bag passed under it. "Hold onto me, so I can reach...out...just...a..."

Beemer stretched himself out over the river, dangerously close to falling in himself. At the last moment, he felt Jaso's reassuring grasp on his hind legs. He had to time his final lunge just right...just as the bag passed within a few inches of him. It was too far. He couldn't make it. The image of an irate Bulldog chewing off his ears flashed in his mind. Doggin would take only too much pleasure in making him pay for losing Allie on her first mission. At the last second, Beemer yelled back to Jaco, "Let me go!"

As soon as he felt Jaco ease up, he coiled his powerful rear legs and leapt into the water, landing on the now soaked bag.

"Gotcha," he yelled just before taking on a mouthful of water. Now, what in the hell have I done, he wondered, as the bag dipped below the surface, threatening to drown both cats. Holding onto the bag with his front claws, he kicked with all his might with his back legs. As they reached the surface again, he shouted to Allie, "I've got you, Allie. Just stay calm and do whatever you can to stay afloat." He looked towards the shore where he found Jaco following his journey down the river. He knew the old wives' tale that cats couldn't swim wasn't true. It's just that cats hated the water, so they did everything they could to avoid it. He heard Allie's pleading meow, and it spurred him on, even though he was already tiring as he fought to keep the two of them afloat.

The next few minutes his entire focus was on survival and keeping Allie and his head above water. He lost all track of time or how far they traveled or whether or not Jaco was even still with him on the shore. He felt his strength weakening and felt lightheaded from oxygen deprivation. If he blacked out it would be all over for both of them, so he shook himself to stay conscious, but it didn't seem to help. It was just delaying the inevitable. He was about to die.

"Hang on, Beemer," Jaco called from shore. "I've almost got you."

The sound of his friend's voice was like a cold spray of water on his face, or maybe it was the actual cold spray of water that woke him up. He looked around. They were nearing an outcropping of rocks, and out in the center of it stood Jaco. Somehow, he'd leapt from rock to rock until he positioned himself near where Beemer was headed. With his last ounce of strength, he struggled towards the rocks, and slowly made headway. With his last kick, his legs contacted something under the water. A rock—solid ground. With weak, trembling legs, and with help from Jaco, he pulled Allie and himself out of the water and onto the rocks where he collapsed.

It was close to dawn when the three water-soaked cats slowly made their way back to Doggin's hideout, passing along the way of the two-legs' large vessels. With only mild interest, Beemer glanced at the ship. "Where do the two-legs go in those things?" he asked though he really didn't expect Jaco to know.

"Why, it takes them to America!" Jaco replied with enthusiasm. "One of these days I'm going to jump on one of those ships and go there myself, I am, I am. I hear those ships are filled with mice and rats. Plenty of food for catters like you and me. Whatta you say, want to go with me on an adventure?"

"No way," Beemer replied. "I'm a Londoner true blue. Besides, I've had more than enough adventure for one day. Enough to last a year or more."

"How about you, Allie? Ever thought what life in America would be like?" Jaco asked, but he could hardly get a word out of the waterlogged Allie, who just shook her head, mortified by the trouble she had caused.

No one spoke again until they were within sight of Doggin's place. "Let me do all the talking," Beemer said, as they made they way down the steps that led to the basement of the pub that Doggin's two-legs owned and where Doggin served as one of the bouncers. Doggin was one of the largest and meanest Bulldogs Beemer had ever had the misfortune to run into, but as long as you stayed on the dog's good side, and did his bidding, he'd leave you alone. The only problem there seemed to be a lot more room on his bad side than his good, so Beemer and the others of the cat clan were constantly fighting among themselves to be one of the few that Doggin would leave alone.

Jaco nodded. He was more than happy to let Beemer lead the way. After all, he seemed to have a way with Doggin that no one quite understood, so he figured if anyone could talk themselves out of trouble it would be Beemer.

Allie wasn't so sure. "I have something that…"

"I don't want to hear a peep out of you, do you hear?" Beemer stopped and stared at her hard. "You've done quite enough for one day. Doggin might have taken a fancy to you early on, but I can assure you that his temperament changes faster than the direction of the wind. So, shuddup and let me do the talking."

Allie opened her mouth as though to disagree, but noticing the look on Jaco's face, decided it best to stay quiet… at least for the moment. The three of them snuck down the final few steps only to run smack dab into Doggin as he was about to leave.

"Well, look at what the cats drug in… their own scrawny, soaked caucuses. Where in the hell have you been — bathing in the Thames?"

Beemer stepped forward as Jaco hid behind the large orange tabby. Allie tried to step in front of Beemer, but he deftly pushed her away. "We had a bit of a run in with the two-legs but all have been put to the right now. Sorry to be so long in getting back. What did you think of the haul? Pretty nice for a night's work, wouldn't you say?"

Doggin scoffed. "I wouldn't say. I mean the loot was okay, but you alerted the two-legs. Now they're all up in arms about a new gang of burglars. Our best defense was our ability to fly under their watchful eyes. Now, you've gone and blown it. And I hear that you almost lost our new recruit to them as well."

Beemer glanced over to Allie despite himself. It would be so easy to simply turn it all back on her. After all, it had been her fault for not obeying his orders, but that wasn't his style. If he turned her over to Doggin then he'd lose the trust of all the other cats, and that would never do. They all depended on each other for their survival. No, better to take Doggin's wrath on his own shoulders this time.

"I'm sorry, Doggin," Beemer replied, hunching his shoulders and looking as docile and submissive as possible. "It won't happen again. You can cut my rations in half if you want as my punishment."

"I've already cut them into thirds," Doggin replied, "For your entire crew. And that's just for starters. I'm sure I can think up some other ways to teach you a lesson in the coming days."

"I have something that might help," Allie said softly as she stepped around Beemer and smiled at Doggin. "May I show you?"

"Allie, what did I..." Beemer started but was interrupted by Doggin.

"Why, the little cat does know how to talk. What do you have to say for yourself?"

"Only this," Allie replied as she hunched over and began to cough and gag.

"What the...?" Doggin said as he stepped back alarmed.

"Must be a hairball," Jaco replied.

Allie ignored them but continued to gag and retch until finally, she coughed up a volume of water left over from the Thames...and the brilliant diamond ring she'd stolen.

"What is that?" Doggin asked once he'd regained his composure, staring at the pool of water with the ring in its center.

"It's a babble," Allie replied just barely audibly. "It's easily worth 5 times the amount of food we pilfered last night. I dare say we couldn't steal as much food as this could be traded for in three months of nightly raids, not to mention how much attention that many raids would bring down on us. But if we just stole a bauble or two a month like this one, we'd all be sitting pretty for the rest of our lives."

"You don't say?" Doggin replied, suddenly taking a renewed interest in what lay before him. "You know, I've seen these on some of the wealthier two-legs, now that you mention it. They do seem to like their babbles, as you call them. "Where did you find it?"

Allie opened her mouth as though to answer, then paused. "Well, we'll talk about that," she replied as she reached over pushed the ring out of the pool of water and towards Doggin. This is yours, in exchange for doubling our rations instead of cutting them."

"Why...are you...?" Doggin blinked several times, apparently shocked by Allie's reply, then he chuckled darkly. "I think our new recruit might just be a keeper." He picked up the ring in his mouth where he hung on one of his lower canines. "Keep a close eye on her, Beemer. I'm holding you responsible if anything happens to her."

"Yes, sir," Beemer replied, stunned by the turn of events himself. "She'll not leave my sight, day or night."

* * *

Over the next year, Doggin's coffers grew richer as did his whims and desires for more. With it, Allie's and Beemer's alliance grew stronger as well. Allie's size, shape, color, and prowess made her the perfect burglar. She was small for her age, slender and coal black. She could slide through the night on her soft cat pads without detection which her sinewy frame gave her incredible leaping abilities. Meanwhile, Beemer ran the support crew, who would assist Allie in the break-ins. It was no longer necessary to steal food from the pantries of the rich. Instead, they focused on their "baubles" — mostly jewelry of the rich ladies, and tried to keep their missions down to only one or two per month, despite Doggin's insistence that they could pull in more loot by expanding their territory and their frequency of raids.

Allie and Beemer realized the danger of too many raids. Already, the two-legs knew something had invaded their secure homes and were taking actions to try to protect their valuables. The security was becoming tighter and tighter and more and more homes were guarded not only by the police but more dangerous for Allie and her crew, by a rash of Dobermans and other guard dogs.

Overall life was good for Doggin and his cat clan, with Beemer and Allie on top of it all. "This life might be a dung heap," Beemer said frequently, "but at least you and I are on top of the heap." Allie had to reluctantly agree their lives were far better than the other stray animals of London, where most of them had to depend on scrounging what they could from the garbage or begging for scraps from the rear entrances of stores and other pubs. The contrast started playing on Allie's conscience more and more as the gap between their lives and those of the other animals grew larger until one day she could stand it no longer.

"Beemer, can I ask you a question?" She asked one day after the two of them had enjoyed a particularly rich and filling meal and were lounging around the basement of the pub.

"Sure, what is it, my fine feline friend?"

Surprised that she'd caught him in such a good mood, she suddenly didn't know quite what the question was she wanted to ask. She finally decided on the direct approach. "Do you ever worry about all the other stray animals that don't have it as good as we have it?"

"Honestly, no," Beemer replied. "Why should I? We're the ones who take the risk to live the life we do. We're the ones that end up in a canvas bag tossed into the Thames if we're caught."

Allie shuddered at the reminder. It hadn't been the only close call she'd had in the past year. By her calculation, she'd easily used up at least three of her ten lives. At this rate, she'd be lucky to make it to three or four, but then again, few feral animals lived more than a couple of years, often succumbing to disease or starvation long in the first couple of years. Three or four would be considered old age by most stray's standards.

"Yes, I understand that we're the ones who take the risks so should reap most of the rewards, but still, don't you think we could maybe help out at least a few of the less fortunate."

Beemer, who'd been stretched out on his bag on a stack of old canvas bags, opened one eye and stared at Allie. "You can't be serious," he replied. "Can you imagine what Doggin would do if he found out we were giving to the poor? He'd skin both of our hides and hang them out on the pub sign to dry."

He wouldn't dare skin my hide, Allie thought. I'm too important to him and the system he had going. But she decided it wouldn't be wise to point that out to Beemer, so instead replied, "Yes, I guess you're right. I'm sure you know best."

"Of course I do. Now, don't worry your pretty little head about it anymore. We need to rest up. Our next excursion is tomorrow."

Allie tried to do what he asked but found the images of starving and abused animals wouldn't let her sleep. Finally, around three in the morning, she dozed off...

...And found herself lying in the same position she'd fallen asleep, but instead of an old canvas bag beneath her, she found herself lying on a billowing cloud colored a soft lavender, and as she looked around, she saw standing in front of her an equally lavendered gazelle.

"Hello, Allie," the gazelle said. "I'm Grace. Pleasant dreams?"

"Huh? What?" Allie replied as she shook herself. "Am I dreaming?"

"I don't know, are you?" Grace asked back. "Does it really matter?"

"No, I guess not, as long as I wake up and I'm back where I belong."

"Well, that's what I want to talk with you about?" Grace laid down so she was closer to the same level with the smaller animal. "We've been picking up signals from you that you're growing increasingly aware of the suffering of other animals."

"We? We who?"

"I'm on the Council of the Spiritual Frontier. We oversee the entire animal kingdom, and we too have grown increasingly concerned with the plight of the animals of Earth. We have developed a plan to take a more proactive role to try to combat some of the abuses and inequities we're observing that are happening as a consequence of the increase in the human species — the two legs as I believe you refer to them. We think you may play an important part in our plan."

"Me?" Allie replied, dumbfounded by the whole idea. "Why me? I'm no one. I'm just a stray cat working to stay alive just like the countless other feral animals. What difference could I possibly make?"

"Yes, that is a good question to ask yourself? Grace replied. "Here's another one. What difference do you want to make?"

Allie didn't know how to answer that question, so she just stared back at the gazelle. Finally, she decided to try a different tact. "What's this plan of yours?"

"Oh, I'm not at liberty to tell you that...not yet. But let me ask you this. What if you could make a real difference with the thousands and thousands of animals that are suffering on earth now? Oh, I don't mean you could eliminate all suffering, but you could ease the burden for some, maybe even for many, would you?" Grace looked at Allie with a penetrating stare.

"Well, yes, I suppose so...sure. Who wouldn't?"

"Many," Grace said. "Unfortunately, far too many, I'm afraid. But not you, right? Would you be willing to dedicate your life to it — to a life of selfless service?"

"Whoa, wait just a minute," Allie said as she felt the question grip her heart, and she could feel herself backing away from the gazelle.

"Why would I do that?" She finally asked, unsure what else to say and figuring she might gain the advantage by asking her own question.

"For the opportunity to live a life that truly matters," Grace replied unperturbed. "Oh, it wouldn't be an easy life for sure. It would have as much danger and risk as your current life, and even more adventure. The main difference is that you'd be helping out many other animals, not just yourself."

Allie thought about what Grace had said for a moment before replying, "You know you're one hell of a negotiator. You want me to give up the life I have now for even more risk, more danger, and for what? So, I can say my life mattered? What kind of deal is that?"

"The best deal you could ever hope to make," Grace replied softly, "if you're the kind of cat I think you are."

This is a ridiculous dream, Allie thought as she tried to wake herself up, but try as she did, she remained there on the cloud trying her best not to look at Grace the gazelle as the questions continued to nag at her. If she was totally honest with herself, there was something about the gazelle's offer that was strangely, maybe insanely, attractive. She finally met Grace's gaze.

"Can I have a few days to think about it?"

"Sure, the ship doesn't sail until the first of the week," Grace replied with a light smile.

"What ship?"

"The ship you need to be on that leaves for the America on Sunday. If you accept my offer, you need to be on it. Your first mission is on the other side of the Atlantic." And with that declaration the lavender gazelle evaporated from sight, the clouds following a moment later. Allie felt herself falling and jerked awake, finding herself once more lying beside Beemer on the canvas bag.

Beemer opened one eye to stare at her.

"Are you okay?"

Allie started to tell him about the strange dream but at the last minute thought better of it. Instead, she replied, "Yeah, just a bad dream. Must have eaten too many sausages." She turned back over to go back to sleep, but the haunting questions kept her awake the rest of the night.

* * *

Despite a restless night, by the time dawn broke, Allie had convinced herself it was just a silly dream — one she intended to forget as soon as possible.

Unfortunately, it wasn't that easy. When Beemer and she went out to case the location for their next heist, everywhere she looked all she could see was the terrible plight of so many animals, from the abused workhorses struggling to pull overly full carts while their ribs stuck out with each heaving breath, to the mongrel dogs and feral cats that were to be found on every street and down the dark alleys where they scratched out a meager existence.

While she tried to turn a blind eye to it all, Grace's word continued to haunt her. It wouldn't be an easy life for sure. It would have as much danger and risk as your current life, and even more adventure. The main difference is that you'd be helping out many other animals, not just yourself.

"Shuddup already," she finally thought, then realized the startled look on Beemer's face that she'd actually screamed it out loud.

"What's up with you, kiddo?" Beemer asked as they neared the two story house of Lord and Lady Lawthrop, repudiated to be one of the most affluent couples in the southern part of London. Doggin had received words from one of his sources that the Lawthrops would be at a party on Saturday night, leaving the house and most of Mrs. Lawthrop's jewels unattended except for the servants who would be asleep in the basement.

"Oh nothing," Allie replied, embarrassed by her outcry. "Just that crazy dream I had last night. Spooked me out a bit. I'll be fine. Let's get this done. I need to get at least one good night of sleep before we pull this off."

"Okay," Beemer replied but continued to look concern. "You need to get your head in the game. We've got a lot riding on this one. I just got word from Doggin that he expects this to be the largest heist ever. Evidently, he needs it to cover some gambling debts."

"You've got to be kidding?" Allie replied, suddenly more angry than embarrassed. "We're risking our necks so we can cover a delinquent Bulldog's gambling debts? What is this world coming to?"

"Ours is not to ask such questions." Beemer stopped and turned towards her. "We've got a pretty sweet deal going on here. Let's not blow it. We could be out on the street like all these other poor beasts. You wouldn't want that would you?"

Before she could reply, Beemer continued. "Besides, I got plans for us. I was thinking, it's about time you and I quit pretending there's not something going on with us, and go ahead and give in to our natural instincts and drives."

Allie stared at him with a mixture of disbelief, confusion, and surprise on her face. "What are you talking about?"

"You know what I'm talking about. Letting nature take its course." Beemer suddenly looked a little embarrassed himself. "You and I will make beautiful babies, Allie, and with my size and your smarts, they'll be a whole new breed."

"What in the world makes you think I would ever agree to bring a litter into this world that's already over crowded with unloved and abused animals?"

"Well, because it's what we do," Beemer replied simply. "It's what we've always done."

The rest of the day went downhill from there. Allie continued to see the plight of the animal kingdom everywhere she turned, except now she also thought she saw her own babies mixed into the horrors of the London streets. To make matters worse, every so often she thought she'd see a flicker of lavender out of the corner of her eye but every time she turned in that direction it would disappear. She began to think she must be going insane and wondered if the high meat diet Beemer and she had been on lately might be laced with something.

She ate only lightly that night, then begged off from the typical night of caterwauling so she could go to bed early. She really needed some sleep before tomorrow's caper.

But it proved to be another restless night made worse by a visit from Grace.

"Hello, Allie. It's good to talk with you again. What have you decided?"

Allie looked around her to discover that she was once again among the lavender clouds.

"Am I dreaming?" She asked again.

"I don't know, are you?" Grace asked back. "Does it really matter?"

"You know, you're pretty good at avoiding my questions."

Grace smiled and nodded. "And yet, I'm the one who asked the first question that you've not yet answered. What have you decided?"

Allie hung her head for a moment, wondering if there was some way to put off this conversation. When she realized there wasn't, she looked up and answered, "I'll do it…even though I don't really understand what I'm agreeing to do," she finished with an edge to her voice.

"That's right you don't," Grace replied. "Here's all you need to know at this point. Be on the Intrepid tomorrow by noon. That's when it's scheduled to leave port. I'll fill you in more tomorrow."

Allie nodded slowly. "You know, you're asking me to take a lot on faith. Change my whole life around. Don't you think you could give me a little more to go on."

"No," Grace replied. "Faith and trust are all we have sometimes. You'll get used to it." And with that, she was gone, and Allie was once again back on earth sleeping in the pub's basement. She sat up and looked around at the rest of the crew that had become her family…the family that she was about to let down. But the decision had been made and even though she didn't like it, she knew it was the right one. Spying Jaco sleeping in his customary place, she tip-toed over to him and shook him awake.

"I need to see you outside," she said, then walked towards the door.

"Huh, what? You mean now?" Jaco replied with a sleepy shake of his head.

Allie nodded but didn't say anything else until the two of them were outside.

"It's time," she said.

"What? Are you asking me what time it is? I haven't the foggiest—sleeping time is all I know." Jaco replied.

"No, itchit, I said it's time…time for you to go solo…tomorrow night on the heist."

"Whoa, there now, Allie. I really appreciate your show of confidence in me, but I'm hardly ready to pull off a heist on my own…especially not the most important one of the year."

"Yes, you are. You have to be because…"Allie paused. Do I dare tell him the truth, she wondered. Probably a bad idea but she didn't know what else to say. "…I won't be there tomorrow. I'll be on my way to America."

"You'll what? No way! But that's my dream."

"So, do you want to go with me?" Allie asked.

"Huh, no…not really," Jaco replied. "I mean, one day I might want to go, but well…okay, you're right. It's not something I'll ever really do. It's just fun to talk about it. But you? Why are you going?"

"I have another mission I've been assigned."

"By who — Doggin, or Beemer?"

"Neither," Allie replied. "Listen, it's a long story and too complicated to get into now. The point is that I need you to cover for me. I know you can do it. I'll be eternally grateful."

Jaco stood frozen in place. Finally, he shook himself out of his stupor and smiled at Allie. "Okay, if you say I'm ready then I'm ready. I'll just have to have faith and trust what you say."

The comment stunned Allie. "How did you…have you been talking…? Oh, never mind. Just thank you, Jaco…and thanks for being my friend. I'm going to miss you."

"Yeah, I'll miss you too, but hey, you go get yourself settled in America and who knows, maybe I'll come visit you one day."

The two of them nuzzled against each other for a moment before returning to the pub.

The next morning around eleven Allie told Beemer that she needed to go out to get a few things for the heist that evening. She felt terrible about lying to him but didn't know any other way to handle it. As she started to leave, she looked back at the pub's basement that had been her home for most of her life. I'm going to miss this place, she thought as she looked around. And I'm going to miss this misfit of a family too. She glanced over where Beemer was eating a late breakfast of fish. And I'm going to miss you most of all even with your crazy idea of starting a family. She sighed. Change, even what she hoped would be a positive change was hard.

As she felt a tear start to build in her eyes, she sniffed it under control and turned and walked away. Outside, and free she strutted along the familiar streets on her way to the docks. She'd made it a point to find where the Intrepid was docked earlier so she wouldn't have to wander around trying to find it. Sure enough, it was evident that the sailors were in the last stages of preparing to leave. And there on deck were several crates with bars and within each one was a large animal — a lion in one, a bear in another, and next to that one was a lavender gazelle.

It's Grace! Allie almost yelled to her, but then thought better of it. What was she doing in a cage? Was she a part of the circus that was being loaded for their trip to America?

Grace saw her at the same moment and waved to her then pointed towards the stern of the ship where a thick rope was still tied to the pier. But unlike the other ropes that had circular guards to keep rats and other varmints from climbing on board, this one was clear. Obviously, Grace had been at work already.

Allie quietly snuck on board and made her way to Grace's cage. "What are you doing caged like a wild animal?" She asked.

"Sometimes, my dear, the best way to stay hidden is to be right out in the open," Grace replied. "The cage fits my purpose for now. You're just in time. See that man there in the trench coat wearing the black armband?"

Allie looked in the direction Grace was pointing and nodded. "Yes, I see him."

"He's your mission," Grace continued. "His name is Henry. He's on the final leg of a European journey and is now returning home to America. He's wearing the black armband because he's in mourning over what he observed while in Europe. Your job is to convince him that the idea that he's been mulling over in his mind, is one worth pursuing.

"How am I to do that?" Allie asked.

"By talking him into it," Grace replied. "So step just a little closer."

Allie did as she was told but then jumped back as the large gazelle raised one of her front hooves.

"Stand still," Grace ordered. "I'm not going to hurt you. I just need to touch you for this next part."

Allie started to ask her a question, then thought better of it. She'd probably only get some cryptic answer anyway.

As Grace placed her hoof on Allie's head, she felt a strange sensation like a wave of energy passing between the two of them, then nothing...except for the sounds around her began to change. The chatter of human voices that had been mixed with the sounds of the busy pier changed. Suddenly, it wasn't senseless chatter but sounds that she could understand.

"What did you just do to me?"

"I just gave you a small gift," Grace replied, "the gift of human language. You'll now be able to understand Henry and just as important, he'll be able to understand you."

Allie stepped back away from Grace, a stunned look on her face. "You can do that...just with a wave of your hoof?"

"Oh dear, you have no idea what all I'm capable of," Grace said with a chuckle. "Now, back to business. Henry must carry on with his idea, and you must be sure that he does. And if he does, you will have passed your test."

"What idea...?" Allie started, then changed course. "What test? I've got to pass a test? You didn't tell me anything about a test."

"One way to view life is that it's simply a series of tests...and hopefully, we learn from all of them. You've already passed the test to trust and have faith, so let's not have to repeat that one right now."

"Well, what do I get if I pass this next test?" Allie asked, finding herself becoming annoyed at Grace again, and wanting to change the subject.

"You will be admitted," Grace replied.

"Admitted? Admitted to what?"

But Grace was no longer paying attention to her, but instead pointed again at Henry. "There he goes. You better catch up. This is a large ship. If you lose sight of him, it could take you days to locate him again."

"But...what?" Allie started, then seeing that Grace was right, ran after the tall man with the black armband. "This conversation isn't finished," she said over her shoulder, but Grace and her cage were nowhere to be seen.

Allie trailed behind Henry at a safe distance staying in the shadows and out from under other people's feet as much as possible. She followed him to his room, then stationed herself outside his door, waiting for the right time to make her initial contact.

And when would that be, she wondered. When could she, a four-leg approach a two-leg for a casual conversation about following your dreams? This is ridiculous, she thought. I'll totally freak him out, he'll call the purser and have me thrown from ship...of course, after we're out to sea. I can swim but all the way back to shore? The more she analyzed her situation, the worse it became.

The opportunity came later in the evening after she'd followed Henry to dinner where he ate and drank...but mostly drank his dinner, having several glasses of red wine, followed up with champagne, and finishing off with an aperitif. As he made his way back to his room, Allie noticed he staggered and swayed a few times, and it wasn't just due to the movement of the ship. Henry was drunk.

Which made it a perfect time to talk to him, at least in Allie's mind. She found it easy to slip into his room behind him, where she hid under his bed as he prepared for sleep, pulling out a flask from a drawer and pouring himself another drink. He retired to bed with the drink and a book, although he didn't bother to open it, but laid in bed sipping on his brandy.

After a minute or two, when it was clear he'd settled in for the evening, Allie decided she'd better speak up before he fell asleep or passed out and couldn't be woken.

She didn't know quite how to begin so she simply started humming a song she often sang to herself at night to help her rest up. She started as softly as she could then slowly built up in volume, hoping to not startle him out of his skin. It seemed to work.

"Hello there, what's this? Piped in music is it?" He said as he turned to find the source of the sound.

"No, not quite," Allie replied, crawling out from under the bed where she'd been hiding and jumping on the desk next to the bed.

"Holy Mother of..." Henry shouted, leaping out of bed, crossing himself as he did so. "What's this? Am I hallucinating?" He glanced at the drink in his hand and placed it gently on the floor. "Enough of that for this evening."

"No, you're not hallucinating, and I'm not a spirit, just a cat...well, a cat who has been sent to you to...to help you with your idea." Allie didn't quite know what to say, so she just said what came to mind first.

"My idea? Really?" Henry said, as he sat down on the edge of the bed and stared at her. "What about my idea? If you've come to try to talk me out of it…"

"No, not at all," Allie interrupted. "On the contrary. I think it's a splendid idea, and I'm here to encourage you to take immediate action on it when you arrive home…no matter what others have said."

"Oh, I see. You like the idea, huh? Well, I guess that figures. After all, you're an animal. What's not to like?"

"Pardon?" Allie said, confused by his comment. What did her being an animal have to do with it? "Oh well, yes, of course, my being an animal might explain it, or it might simply be a great idea. Perhaps you could share with me some more of the details." After all, she thought, it would be a lot easier to enroll him into taking action if I knew what the hell I was talking about.

"Well sure, I guess," Henry said as he stooped down and picked up his drink to take another sip. "It's really quite simple. You see, I saw so much suffering while touring Europe. Animals of all different species, especially domestic animals that were being abused, poorly cared for, starved and beaten. I mean, I have this money…oh, not a great sum of money, but my father was quite successful with his shipbuilding, and he left me a quite tidy inheritance…far more than I need to live on, so I thought, why not use it for some good." It was obvious that as he talked about his idea, he was growing more enthusiastic about it, as was Allie.

"So, I thought why not start an organization that would be dedicated to relieving such suffering in my own country, for I have seen just as much abuse in America. I've even thought up a name for it. Would you like to hear it?"

"Oh, yes, that would be great," Allie replied.

"I would call it the American Society for the Prevention of Cruelty to Animals," Henry said, raising his glass to toast the name.

"Why that's…that's a, well, it's a mouth full, that's for sure," Allie said, unsure what else to say. "But it does convey the idea quite well," she added.

"Humm," Henry said, as he mulled over her comment. "You know you're right. It is a mouthful. Perhaps we could simply call it by its letters for short — the ASPCA. How's that?"

"Splendid," Allie replied, now as excited about the idea as Henry. "So, will you do it? Will you start the ASPCA upon your return?"

"Yes, by golly I will," Henry replied, downing his glass and pouring himself another one, and then offering the flask to Allie.

"No thanks, not while I'm working," Allie replied.

"Oh, okay, I understand. Well then, let's shake on it," Henry replied changing his drink to the other hand and holding out his right one.

Having seen other humans shake on various deals, Allie held out her paw.

"Other one," Henry corrected.

"Oh, sorry." She held out her right paw and they shook on it.

"Now, you've promised me that you'll proceed no matter what anyone else says, right?"

"Yes, I have and one thing you can count on when Henry Bergh makes a promise, he keeps it. Besides, what kind of cad would I be to go back on my word that I gave to a talking cat?

* * *

"Wow, that's incredible," Zak said as Sampson finished his story. "You mean, Ra-Kit was instrumental in convincing Henry Bergh to start the ASPCA on her first mission?"

"Well, like I said, that's the official story straight from the Spiritual Frontier and I have no reason to not believe it," Sampson replied.

"So, what happened after that?" Zak asked.

"Well, it took a few months after Henry returned to New York to complete the process. But he was as good as his word even though he continued to get a lot of static from his friends and associates. And not long after that Allie was admitted into the elite ranks of magic cats. That's when she became Ra-Kit."

"And is it true that her longevity is due to the fact that all the other cats have agreed to donate one of their ten lives to the clan of the magic cats, and that since she'd the last living member of the clan she gets them all?"

"Yes, that's true," Sampson replied. "It may be next to impossible to herd cats, but when it comes to making a difference, cats all over the world have been very generous with their life energy which has allowed Ra-Kit to continue to serve the animal kingdom for over a hundred and fifty years."

"That's really something," Zak said. "And to think, she doesn't look a day over seventy-five."

He stared at Sampson for a long moment before they both broke down laughing.

About the Author
W. Bradford Swift

W. Bradford Swift is a former veterinarian turned author. Swift became an avid reader of fantasy and science fiction as an eleven-year-old boy when his next-door neighbor, a children's librarian, took pity on his single-parent mom. Bored out of his gourd with no one to play with but good 'ol mom, he drove her crazy. Then Mrs. Crabtree brought home a stack of books she knew would hook a young boy's imagination and give his mother some relief. It worked. Swift has been hooked ever since.

Swift lives in the "Paradise Found" of the North Carolina mountains with his wife, daughter, and a menagerie of four-legged family members.

Books by W. Bradford Swift:

Dominion Over All (book 1 of the Zak Bates Eco-adventure series)
Endangered (book 2 of the Zak Bates Eco-adventure series)
Amberlin: Divine Destiny (book 1 of the Amberlin series)
Spacehoppers
Spiral of Fulfillment

Lightning Source UK Ltd.
Milton Keynes UK
UKHW041853190121
377353UK00001B/116